PRAISE FOR KELLIE COATES GILBERT

"If you're looking for a new author to read, you can't go wrong with Kellie Coates Gilbert."
~**Lisa Wingate**, NY Times bestselling author of *Before We Were Yours*

"Well-drawn, sympathetic characters and graceful language"
~**Library Journal**

"Deft, crisp storytelling"
~**RT Book Reviews**

"I devoured the book in one sitting."
~**Chick Lit Central**

"Gilbert's heartfelt fiction is always a pleasure to read."
~**Buzzing About Books**

"Kellie Coates Gilbert delivers emotionally gripping plots and authentic characters."

~Life Is Story

"I laughed, I cried, I wanted to throw my book against the wall, but I couldn't quit reading."
~Amazon reader

"I have read other books I had a hard time putting down, but this story totally captivated me."
~Goodreads reader

"I became somewhat depressed when the story actually ended. I wanted more."
~Barnes and Noble reader

FRIENDS ARE FOREVER

THE TETON MOUNTAIN SERIES
BOOK 6

KELLIE COATES GILBERT

Copyright © 2025 by Kellie Coates Gilbert

All rights reserved.

No part of this book may be reproduced in any form or by any electronic or mechanical means, including information storage and retrieval systems, without written permission from the author, except for the use of brief quotations in a book review.

Cover Design: Kim Killion/The Killion Group

For Lennon Gumdrop
Sometimes your best friend is a three and a half pound yorkie who sits on your lap daily while you are writing. 🩶

ALSO BY KELLIE COATES GILBERT

Dear Readers,

Thank you for reading this story. If you'd like to read more of my books, please check out these series. To purchase at special discounts: www.kelliecoatesgilbertbooks.com

TETON MOUNTAIN SERIES

Where We Belong – Book 1

Echoes of the Heart – Book 2

Holding the Dream – Book 3

As the Sun Rises – Book 4

Losing the Moon – Book 5

Friends are Forever – Book 6

A Teton Mountain Christmas – Book 7

MAUI ISLAND SERIES

Under the Maui Sky – Book 1

Silver Island Moon – Book 2

Tides of Paradise – Book 3

The Last Aloha – Book 4

Ohana Sunrise – Book 5

Sweet Plumeria Dawn – Book 6

Songs of the Rainbow – Book 7

Hibiscus Christmas – Book 8

PACIFIC BAY SERIES

Chances Are – Book 1

Remember Us – Book 2

Chasing Wind – Book 3

Between Rains – Book 4

SUN VALLEY SERIES

Sisters – Book 1

Heartbeats – Book 2

Changes – Book 3

Promises – Book 4

TEXAS GOLD COLLECTION

A Woman of Fortune – Book 1

Where Rivers Part – Book 2

A Reason to Stay – Book 3

What Matters Most – Book 4

STAND ALONE NOVELS:

Mother of Pearl

AVAILABLE AT ALL MAJOR RETAILERS

FOR EXCLUSIVE DISCOUNTS:

www.kelliecoatesgilbertbooks.com

FRIENDS ARE FOREVER
TETON MOUNTAIN SERIES, BOOK 6

Kellie Coates Gilbert

1

Reva Nygard sat at her desk, sipping lukewarm coffee and staring at a framed photo of Lucan. Who knew a three-year-old could run you ragged? And all before eight o'clock in the morning?

Every morning, before the sun crested over the Tetons, little Lucan climbed out of his bed and into hers, his warm, wiggly body tucking against her side, his tiny fingers tracing the curve of her face as he whispered, "*Mama, wake up.*"

Before she could answer, a strong arm would wrap around her waist, pulling her closer, Kellen's deep, sleepy voice murmuring, "*Give your mama a few more minutes, buddy.*" But Lucan, all boundless energy and bright curiosity, never did. He was up and running, calling for pancakes or his favorite dinosaur pajamas. Kellen would sigh with exaggerated defeat before tossing the covers back and rolling out of bed to chase after their son. Reva lay there for a moment longer, listening to their laughter—her boys—before slipping into the kitchen where Kellen was already flipping pancakes, Lucan on his shoulders, giggling at every little movement.

Smiling at the memory, Reva stood and made her way to

the coffee pot on the other side of her office, remembering how Kellen would pull her close, pressing a kiss to her forehead, whispering, "*I love this life we've built.*" And so did she. Because for all the years she had spent being strong for everyone else, it turned out love—true, deep, unconditional love—was what had made her stronger than ever.

After filling her cup with hot coffee, she wandered to the window and gazed out. Thunder Mountain was waking up. The crisp fall morning air carried the scent of pine, the town's heartbeat already pulsing as shopkeepers flipped over "Open" signs and ranch trucks rumbled down Main Street. A couple of early risers strolled along the wooden-planked sidewalk, waving as they passed.

This town. Her town.

Before she was a wife and mother, she'd spent years pouring herself into Thunder Mountain, the tiny community nestled at the base of the Teton Mountains in Wyoming—first as an attorney, and then as mayor.

She knew every pothole, every business owner, and every resident who needed a little extra grace but wouldn't dare ask for it—and she gave it freely. When Merck Taylor, the county assessor, got a little heavy-handed with property valuations, she didn't scold him. Instead, she invited him for coffee, gently steering the conversation toward the town's hardworking families and the burden of rising costs until he sighed, adjusted his numbers, and left with a clearer conscience.

She knew exactly when Fleet Southcott, the town's longtime sheriff, made his rounds and how often he lingered in the Rustic Pine, sipping coffee and swapping stories with Pastor Pete and Annie. She also knew that lately, he'd been forgetting small things—where he left his keys, the name of a longtime resident, a detail from an old case. So, when he paused too long in a conversation or struggled to recall a routine procedure, Reva was quick to step in with a steady hand, a quiet reminder, or a well-placed joke to keep things moving. She never embarrassed him, never called attention to the moments that might sting. Instead, she covered for him when she could, and when she couldn't, she made sure the right people were watching out for him, just like he'd done for the town all these years.

And then there was Larry York, who often got carried away with his conspiracy theories after too many hours online. Rather than dismiss him, Reva listened—really listened—then skillfully redirected him to a community project, making him feel heard while keeping him grounded.

She didn't demand respect. She earned it, one quiet act of grace at a time. And in return—not that she needed any—her own heart was brimming with contentment.

A soft knock on her office door made her jump.

Verna Billingsley, her ever-efficient and always tightly wound assistant, poked her head in. "Your ten o'clock with Mark Dawson to go over the budget for emergency services got moved to eleven, and Fleet just called—something about misplacing an incident file." She sniffed. "He says it's no big deal, but it is a big deal. We don't want city records misplaced."

Reva closed her eyes for a brief second, not wanting to deal with Fleet and his forgetfulness this early in the morning. Instead, she forced a smile. "Anything else?"

"Yes, the girls are waiting for you at the Rustic Pine."

Reva blinked. "Why?"

Verna sighed as though she had better things to do than remind Reva of her own plans. "Because it's Wednesday, and it's what you do. Meet your girlfriends. Drink too much coffee. Solve the world's problems."

Apparently, Fleet wasn't the only one with memory issues this morning. If only she'd had a bit more sleep.

Reva let out a breath and nodded. Right. Wednesday. Their weekly morning coffee at the Rustic Pine, a long-held tradition —that and regular cocktail evenings. Lately, life had been pulling them all in different directions—Charlie Grace with her expanding guest ranch, Capri caught up in returning to work after a protracted recovery and rehab from her accident on the mountain last spring, and Lila balancing the veterinary clinic with a daughter who had found herself facing an unplanned pregnancy.

Reva grabbed her purse and shut down her computer. She turned for the door when her phone buzzed with a text from Charlie Grace. *"We're here. Don't make us come get you."*

Reva let out a quiet chuckle, tossed her phone in her purse, and with squared shoulders followed Verna out of her office.

Some things in life could wait but Wednesday coffee with the same friends who had been by her side since high school wasn't one of them. Besides, if she stalled too long, Charlie Grace would probably send a search party—or worse, Capri.

The last thing she needed was Capri storming into Town Hall—because Capri didn't do subtle. Even when she was newly off crutches.

2

Reva scurried down Main Street, her heels clicking against the wooden sidewalk planks as she made her way toward the Rustic Pine. The early fall air was crisp, tinged with the scent of pine and distant woodsmoke, as she adjusted her blazer and quickened her pace. She had meant to leave the office ten minutes ago, but a last-minute call from a council member about the upcoming road repair project had set her back. Now, she was running even more late to meet the girls at the Rustic Pine. No doubt she'd hear about it.

Halfway across the street, old Mrs. Kellerman flagged her down with frantic waving, a clipboard clutched in her wrinkled hands.

"Mayor Nygard! Just a moment!"

Reva teetered to a sharp halt, her heels scraping against the wooden plank sidewalk as she fought for balance. She turned and forced a polite smile. "Mrs. Kellerman, I—"

"The historical society is submitting a petition to protect the old grain silo from demolition," Mrs. Kellerman said, pushing the clipboard into Reva's hands. "I need your signature to show your support!"

Reva glanced at the clipboard, groaning internally. The grain silo was beyond saving—barely standing, home to raccoons, and a constant safety hazard. "I'll take this back to my office and review it," she said, already stepping backward.

When her declaration met with a disappointed stare, she quickly added, "I promise."

"Thank you, Mayor. That silo's been here longer than I have," Mrs. Kellerman said, almost to herself. "Seen more seasons than I can count, stood through storms that took down barns and fences. My husband used to say a farm wasn't really a farm without one." She paused, lips pressing together before she let out a quiet chuckle. "Truth is, that's where he first kissed me. A long time ago."

Reva granted her a smile. "I'll review the petition and do all I can. You have my word." She patted Mrs. Kellerman on the shoulder. "And sometime, I'd love to hear about that kiss." She winked at the older woman, who smiled before nodding and lumbering away, clutching her shiny black purse.

Before Reva could get away, a stray dog ran right between her legs, knocking her off balance. She yelped, catching herself just before toppling to the pavement, and turned in time to see Albie Barton, the town's ever-nosy newspaper reporter, jotting notes in his ever-present notepad.

"Reva, care to comment on the abandoned pup situation?" Albie asked, stepping in front of her. "I understand little Jewel Nichols found a litter out on the edge of Teton Trails Ranch yesterday."

Reva exhaled sharply. "I'm late, Albie. And this is the first I've heard of it. Sorry."

She sidestepped him and took off again, only to get caught behind a slow-moving tractor rolling down the street.

"Come on," she muttered, practically jogging in place.

When the path finally cleared, she darted across the street, pulled open the Rustic Pine's door, and stepped inside, breathing in the comforting scent of wood, coffee, and grilled bacon. Unlike the rowdy cowboy bar down the street, which attracted the heavy-drinking, line-dancing crowd, the Rustic Pine was a cozy bar and grill run by Pastor Pete and his wife, Annie. With its polished wooden booths, vintage beer signs, and old photographs of Thunder Mountain on the walls, the place felt more like a second home than a business. It was where the locals gathered to swap stories, share meals, and find a little solace after a long day.

Her gaze swept the room, landing on Fleet Southcott, the town's aging cop, perched at the beautiful wooden bar, chatting with Annie. His coffee sat untouched as he animatedly described a movie he'd recently watched.

"...and then this kid—the one with the freckles—he gets lost in a big cornfield, and his dog has to track him down. I tell ya, I didn't see that ending coming." He shook his head. "Those kids...well, they sure get to me." He paused. "Speaking of, why didn't you and Pastor Pete have any?"

Annie tugged the towel from her shoulder and ran it over the bar. "Well, Fleet—it wasn't because we didn't want any. We tried. I guess the good Lord just had other plans for me and Pete."

Fleet sighed, nodding. "Yeah, yeah, I suppose."

Reva spotted her friends at their usual corner table and hurried over. Charlie Grace, Capri, and Lila were all nursing steaming mugs of coffee, their conversation in full swing.

"There she is," Lila teased, nudging a fresh cup of coffee toward Reva as she slid into her seat. "You run into half the town on your way here?"

"Don't ask," Reva grumbled, gratefully taking a sip.

Capri leaned in with a wide grin. "So, Charlie Grace was just filling us in on how the guest ranch expansion is going."

Charlie Grace's eyes lit up. "Yes, it's been a whirlwind. With the new cabins, we'll have space for nearly triple the guests.

And that's not counting the new lodge that's in the planning stages. Oh, and we're considering putting in a pool. Of course, that thrilled Jewel." She paused. "I'm not sure how easy it is to maintain a pool in the harsh winters we have here in the Tetons. But we'll figure it all out. Nick's been helping coordinate the logistics, and the TV show exposure has been insane."

"That's amazing," Lila said. "You deserve all this good fortune."

Reva rested her elbows on the table, her expression thoughtful. "Charlie Grace's expansion isn't just altering the guest ranch—it's changing Thunder Mountain. Ever since that TV show put us on the map, more people have been showing up, not just for a vacation but to stay and make Thunder Mountain their home. Businesses are busier, new shops are opening, and folks are even buying up property. Not everyone loves the idea of our quiet little town getting more attention, but most see the benefits. More jobs, a stronger economy—it's giving people a reason to stick around instead of moving away. Growth like this doesn't come easy, but it means Thunder Mountain isn't just some forgotten spot on the map anymore. We're becoming something bigger."

Annie arrived with a pot of coffee, expertly topping off their cups. The rich aroma filled the air as she gave each of them a smile. "Looks like you girls are busy solving the world's problems," she said, her voice warm and familiar.

"Not yet," Reva quipped, wrapping her hands around the fresh cup. "But give us time."

Charlie Grace lifted her mug in thanks. "You always know exactly when we need a refill, Annie. You've got some kind of sixth sense for it."

Annie chuckled as she propped a hand on her hip, her eyes twinkling with amusement. "I just know my regulars."

Capri gave her an appreciative nod. "We'd be lost without you."

Annie smirked, glancing at Reva. "Well, I'll leave the heavy lifting to the mayor, but at least I can keep everyone caffeinated."

Annie turned her attention to Capri. "So, Nicola was in yesterday. Everyone's wondering when the big wedding day is planned. And by everyone, I mean Nicola Cavendish." She laughed.

Capri shrugged, a playful glint in her eye. "No date set, but don't worry—you all will be the first to know when there's something to mark on the calendar."

As soon as Annie had returned to the bar and was out of earshot, Capri took a sip and sighed. "I swear, if one more person asks when Jake and I are getting married—"

Charlie Grace grinned and gave her a slight elbow jab. "So, when's the wedding?"

Capri groaned. "Oh, stop. We're not in a hurry. Jake and I will know when the time is right. And it will be something simple. Quiet and simple."

"Mm-hmm," Reva murmured. "Speaking of weddings..." she smirked, taking a sip of her coffee.

Just like that, their conversation shifted to Jason's wedding—the event everyone in Thunder Mountain was still buzzing about.

"It was the tackiest spectacle I've ever seen," Lila said, shaking her head. "The whole thing was pink and gold. My favorite was the champagne fountain made out of an actual ice sculpture of the bride and groom. Hours into the ceremony and their faces were melting off."

Charlie Grace shuddered. "Don't forget the sparkler send-off. I thought for sure someone's hair was going to catch on fire."

"And the frosting-loaded-six-tier cake was overkill," Lila added, chuckling. "All that glittery gold piping looked more fitting for a Vegas marquee than a wedding."

Reva laughed. "So, Capri, what's your dream wedding, then?"

"Not that," Capri said firmly. "No pink. No gold. Like I said, something understated and quiet."

Reva arched a brow. "Look, friend—I've known you since we were high school cheerleaders. You've never lived a quiet moment in your life."

Capri grinned. "True."

Reva shot a look over at Charlie Grace. "Hey, what's this I hear about Jewel finding some abandoned pups?"

Charlie Grace let out a soft laugh, shaking her head. "You should've seen Jewel's face when she found them—like it was Christmas morning and every present under the tree had her name on it. She was out near the old logging road with Aunt Mo when she heard these tiny yips, and sure enough, tucked in a little hollow under some brush, were those pups. Abandoned, no mama in sight. She scooped them up like they were made of gold and came running back to the ranch, begging to keep them before Mo even had a chance to blink."

"Did someone dump them there?" Reva asked.

Charlie Grace shook her head. "No, I don't think so. There was no box or anything. Aunt Mo said they looked like they hadn't eaten in a while."

She sighed, running a hand through her hair. "I told Jewel we'd have to figure things out, but that we couldn't keep them. But you know my daughter—she's already named them, picked out where they're all going to sleep, and decided what color collars they'll wear. If it were up to her, she'd adopt every last one. We all know that's not possible." She slid her fingers around her coffee mug. "And for the record, the pups are sleeping in the barn and not in her bedroom—as disappointing as that was for my daughter."

Lila leaned in. "I can take a look at them, make sure they're healthy," she offered. "See if they're now eating well and thriving, check for any issues."

Reva nodded. "And when it's time, I can put up a notice for adoption. There's always someone in town looking for a good dog." She formed a knowing grin. "Of course, with Jewel, there'll never be a time. She won't ever think they're ready to leave."

Charlie Grace chuckled. "Yeah, well, she's got a heart too big for her own good. But we'll figure it out. Somehow."

Across the room, Fleet suddenly straightened at the bar. "Wait a second," he said, narrowing his eyes. "Where's my donut?"

Annie paused mid-pour. "Fleet, you already ate it."

"No, I didn't," Fleet insisted, looking around suspiciously. "I think someone ate it!"

Annie folded her arms. "Fleet."

"What?"

"You ate it."

Fleet's face scrunched in confusion before realization dawned. "Huh." He scratched his head. "Well. Guess I'll have another."

The girls at the corner table burst into laughter, their warm chatter filling the Rustic Pine as the morning stretched on.

3

Thunder Mountain's City Hall stood as a testament to the town's rugged beginnings—a sandstone relic with creaky floors, tall sash windows, and walls lined with sepia-toned photographs in pine and walnut frames. Each image told a piece of the town's story: cattle drives down Main Street, the original mercantile with flour barrels on the porch, and proud schoolchildren standing in front of a one-room schoolhouse beneath a hand-painted sign that read, "*Fall Term 1894*." Time may have marched on, but the building held fast—weathered, dignified, and dependable.

Reva stepped through the front doors with a familiar blend of purpose and calm, still carrying the quiet warmth of her morning coffee with the girls. The laughter, the teasing and talking over one another, the knowing looks—they grounded her. No matter what chaos awaited her inside these walls, time with her friends always reminded her who she was.

That peace lasted all of ten seconds.

She rounded the corner toward her office, noticing Verna's usually bustling desk was conspicuously empty. Odd.

Her assistant's workspace was a flurry of sticky notes,

labeled folders, and whatever seasonal flair Verna had taped to the edges of her monitor—currently a bouquet of sunflowers and a bouncing scarecrow that wiggled every time someone walked by. But no Verna.

A soft thud and a mild grunt sounded from the open door to the adjacent file room.

Reva narrowed her eyes, stepping cautiously toward the sound. Peeking inside, her jaw dropped.

She gasped as her hand flew to her chest. "Verna Billingsley! What are you doing?"

Verna stood precariously on the third rung of a rickety old ladder, a heavy box of files balanced on one hip like she was hauling laundry. Her feet were bare, toes gripping the splintered wooden step, while her orthopedic shoes sat in a sad little heap on the floor below.

"Get down! You'll fall," Reva snapped, heart lurching as she stepped fully into the room. "And goodness knows, we don't need another claim on the city's insurance policy. Fleet's fender bender last week was enough."

Verna startled at Reva's voice and she nearly lost her grip on the box.

"Oh, for heaven's sake, Reva, you scared the spit right outta me," she huffed, adjusting her stance like she'd done this a hundred times—which, knowing Verna, she probably had.

"Don't change the subject," Reva said, marching toward the ladder with her hands on her hips. "Why are you barefoot, balancing on a ladder with a box bigger than your torso? Are you trying to make my life harder today?"

"I *was* trying to find the missing zoning files for that trout farm application, but apparently, gravity and footwear are working against me," Verna shot back, her voice as dry as Wyoming dust. "I thought I could manage it—graceful as an elk crossing a river."

"Graceful?" Reva raised a brow. "Verna, you are many

things. Graceful is not one of them. You're more like a bison in a gift shop."

Verna sniffed. "I was doing just fine until your hollerin' nearly sent me to Jesus."

Reva grabbed the box from her. "You're not going to Jesus. You're going to the break room for a cup of chamomile and a granola bar before you file a worker's comp claim and I have to explain to the city council why my assistant has a broken femur and no shoes."

Verna clambered down, muttering, "It's always a granola bar with you. One day I'm going to demand a jelly-filled donut. Covered in chocolate and sprinkles."

"You can demand all you want, but you're getting oats and sunshine," Reva said, already heading for her office with the box. "Now go put your shoes back on before someone calls the health department."

Reva stepped into her office and placed the cardboard box on one of the leather chairs by the window, brushing a strand of hair behind her ear as she crossed the room to her desk.

Sliding into her chair, she exhaled slowly, letting the weight of the day settle around her. The glow of her computer screen flickered to life as she powered it on, and soon the soft hum filled the quiet space. She clicked into her inbox and began scrolling through the pile-up of emails—updates from city contractors, a note from Verna marked "Urgent" in all caps, and several notes from long-time residents uneasy with the projected town growth estimates she'd expressed at the community meeting last week.

Her fingers hovered over the keyboard before she began typing a response, her brow furrowed in thought. Thunder Mountain might've been small compared to Jackson and Cheyenne, but there was never a dull moment in the mayor's seat.

She was halfway through drafting a memo to the city

council when her phone buzzed with a Georgia area code she hadn't seen in a while.

Her breath caught.

She reached for her phone and picked up.

"Hey, sugar," came the familiar voice on the other end. Mama's voice was strained, husky, like she'd been crying.

Reva's heart immediately jumped into her throat. "Mama? What's going on?"

"It's Grand Memaw. She's not well, Reva. It came on fast, and it's…serious."

Reva's heart thumped hard. "Serious how?"

"She had some kind of spell—doctor's still trying to figure it out. But she's weak. Confused. She's been asking for you. Over and over." A pause. "You need to come home. Today, if you can."

Reva leaned back in her chair, staring at the framed photo of her son. Her voice barely came out as she squeezed her eyes shut. "She's really that bad?"

"I wish I were being dramatic." Mama's voice broke. "I don't know how much time we've got."

Silence stretched between them.

"I'll get the first flight I can," Reva quickly promised, her eyes filling with tears. "Tell her I'm coming."

4

Morning light slanted through the barn slats, golden and gentle, warming the worn wood and stirring the dust into quiet motion. Charlie Grace paused at the threshold, one hand on the weathered frame, the other pressed to her heart.

Jewel was curled up in a bed of old saddle blankets, her small body forming a protective curve around the bundle of pups tucked close to her chest. She'd made a nest of quilts and straw in the corner, just beneath the old harness hooks where barn swallows nested every spring. All six pups were nestled against her chest and belly, sound asleep. One had its nose tucked under Jewel's chin, another sprawled across her arm like it belonged there.

Charlie stepped inside, her boots brushing the hay. The barn was cool still, holding the hush of early morning. She didn't want to disturb the moment, but her eyes couldn't look away. Jewel was softly humming—off-key and quiet, something she'd made up or borrowed from memory. Her fingers moved slowly through the pups' fur, stroking them like she'd seen Charlie do with colts or sick calves.

"They didn't cry last night," Jewel said without looking up. "I kept my hand on 'em so they weren't scared."

Charlie Grace crouched down beside her. She smoothed a hand over Jewel's tangled curls. "You slept out here?"

Jewel shrugged, not meeting her gaze. "I tried to go back inside. But they were cold." Her young daughter rubbed her fist against her eye and yawned. "Can I stay home from school this morning?"

Charlie Grace lifted a strand of damp hair off her daughter's cheek. "It's Saturday."

"Oh, yeah. I forgot."

"Don't you think you should come in and get some breakfast? Aunt Mo left for Idaho Falls to see her friend, so it's up to you and me to fix the pancakes this morning."

Jewel lifted and gently pulled her arm away from the sleeping pups. "Can I bring them with me?"

Charlie Grace shook her head. "No, baby. These are outside dogs."

"But they're little and we could bring them into the house for just a little while," Jewel argued.

She held out her hand and pulled her daughter into a standing position. "No, baby."

"But they're mine, right?" Jewel looked up at her with those wide, earnest eyes that never failed to undo her. "I found them. That makes 'em mine?"

Charlie hesitated. *Oh, sweetheart.* She'd once said those same words, maybe even in this same barn, when she'd found a wounded jackrabbit and tried to hide it in the pantry to keep it warm. Until her dad discovered the situation and ordered her to carry it back outside.

Two days later, the jackrabbit went missing. It wasn't until a year later that she learned that a coyote had gotten it. She'd loved animals her whole life, too—loved hard and fast and without understanding how things sometimes ended.

Charlie felt something tug deep in her chest, that old ache of love and worry tangled together. Jewel had always had a tender heart, but this was different. She wasn't just playing caretaker. She was attaching—fast and deep.

Against her better instincts, she folded. "Okay, just this once. And only for a little while. Help me carry them inside."

Her daughter's face flooded with delight. "Thanks, Mom." She bent and scooped up two of the pups.

Charlie Grace carried the remaining four as they headed for the house.

"They're doing better today," Jewel told her. "They didn't cry last night at all. I think they like my singing."

"I think they do, too." Charlie Grace swallowed around the tightness in her throat. "Sweetheart, you know we can't keep them, right?"

Her daughter stopped in her tracks. "Yes, we can. I'm taking care of them."

Charlie smiled gently, but her heart dipped. "I know. You're doing a beautiful job. But we can't keep them."

Jewel's head snapped in her direction. "Why not? They need me."

"Because this isn't a kennel, baby. It's a ranch. We've already got enough animals to feed, and a business to run, and guests coming in every week. Six dogs...that's a lot."

"But I found them." Jewel's voice cracked. "They didn't have anyone."

Charlie Grace's breath hitched. *I know, kiddo,* she thought, but didn't say it. Instead, she cupped Jewel's cheek and tried to keep her voice steady. "Lila's coming out this afternoon to check them over. We'll see how they're doing and figure out next steps, okay?"

Jewel's lips pressed into a stubborn line, but she nodded. Her fingers curled protectively around the pups, drawing them closer like she could keep the world out just by holding tight enough.

Charlie didn't push. Not now.

Instead, she leaned and kissed the top of Jewel's head, standing beside her daughter, shoulder to shoulder, and listened to the sound of breathing—six soft puppy snuffles and one determined little heartbeat she loved more than anything in the world.

5

Reva yanked open the second drawer of her tall chest and laid a silk turquoise blouse across the bed, followed by a perfectly pressed pair of cream trousers. She paused, the heels of her shoes pressing softly into the plush carpeted floor as she reached for her cosmetic bag.

She zipped up the side of her garment bag and laid it across the bench at the foot of the bed, then moved quickly but deliberately, tugging open drawers, slipping folded items into a structured leather tote. A pale-blue tank top. Her favorite black slacks. A wrap dress, just in case. Heels—three pairs. She wasn't sure what the next few days would hold, but she refused to be caught off guard.

"She's still hanging on," Kellen said from the doorway, Lucan nestled against his shoulder. "Your mama just texted."

Reva stopped mid-fold, her hand resting on a soft cream cardigan. "I should've been on a plane hours ago," she murmured.

"You're going now," Kellen reminded her gently. "The flight schedule out of Jackson is limited. We got you on the first flight available."

She nodded, jaw tight, then moved to her vanity, opening her jewelry case and slipping in a few delicate pieces—pearls, hoops, her grandmother's garnet ring, which she'd worn on special occasions growing up in Georgia.

Their bedroom glowed with soft morning light, filtered through the tall windows that stretched to the beamed ceiling. Beyond the glass, pine trees swayed beneath a breeze that hadn't yet burned off the mountain chill. Reva had designed this home to blend luxury with nature, and in moments like this—when her insides spun—its stillness helped steady her.

"She's asking for me," Reva said quietly, slipping her laptop into her carry-on. "Lucan's never even met her, Kellen. I just...I don't want to lose her before I've said everything I need to say."

Kellen crossed the room and wrapped an arm around her waist, careful not to jostle Lucan, who was busy chewing on the edge of his sleeve. "Everything will be okay."

She leaned into his chest for a moment, letting his steadiness anchor her.

"Well, I'd better get going," she finally said.

Outside, the SUV was already running. Reva stood beside it, coat cinched at the waist, bag slung over one shoulder. She kissed Lucan's forehead, inhaling the baby lotion and that scent only toddlers had—Cheerios and sunshine. "You be good for Daddy."

Lucan giggled and patted her cheek.

Kellen wrapped her in a hug. "We've got this here. You focus on your Grand Memaw. In the meantime, I'll keep our little guy in one piece," Kellen promised. "You keep in touch."

"Every day," she said, voice catching.

She opened the car door, glanced back once more. Lucan waved a pudgy hand, face lit up with the joy of a morning adventure, unaware his mama's heart was splintering. Reva gave one final wave, climbed in, and pulled away from the curb, her designer sunglasses hiding the tears she couldn't blink away.

Soon, the highway unspooled ahead of her like a silver ribbon, winding through pine-covered hills still cloaked in early fog. Reva kept one hand on the wheel, the other resting near her coffee, barely touched. The drive out of Thunder Mountain was always beautiful, but today, it blurred at the edges—her thoughts drifting far from the peaks around her.

Grand Memaw.

The woman had been made of grit and grace in equal measure. She wore cotton dresses and wide straw hats and carried herself like a queen, even when she was shucking pecans or tending to her flower garden in the Georgia heat. Reva could still picture her standing on the wraparound porch of the old farmhouse, a dishrag tossed over one shoulder, her hands dusted with flour while sharing wisdom. "Tell the truth, baby girl," she'd always say, "even when your knees are knocking."

That voice had lived in Reva's head for decades, especially in courtrooms and council chambers, when nerves pressed like a weight against her lungs.

Reva blinked, eyes stinging. She hadn't heard Grand Memaw's voice in months—not really. And now it might be too late.

She tapped the steering wheel gently with her thumbs, the road ahead a blur of memory and fear. She didn't know what she'd find when she pulled into Sweet Briar Grove. She only knew one thing—she couldn't lose Grand Memaw without one more porch swing conversation, one more hug that smelled like lavender powder and home.

6

Charlie Grace stabbed the shovel into the wheelbarrow, the sharp scent of compost rising with the afternoon warmth. A light steam curled off the heap of aged manure and straw, proof the rich fertilizer was still warm from the pile behind the barn. She worked in rhythm, flipping scoops over the rows of withered vines and brittle stalks, remnants of a summer that had given more than it had taken.

Tomato vines, now limp and brown, had once been heavy with crimson orbs—big juicy slicers, sweet yellow cherries, and thick-walled romas that Aunt Mo swore made the best sauce. Over in the far bed, where beans had run wild across a handmade trellis, empty tendrils clung like brittle fingers. The snap peas were long gone, but Charlie Grace could still taste their crisp sweetness, plucked fresh and dipped in hummus on the porch while Jewel ran barefoot through the grass.

She paused to wipe a strand of hair from her cheek, mentally picturing the stacked mason jars in the pantry. Rows of pickled beets, dilly beans, and Aunt Mo's famous sweet corn relish lined the shelves, their colors promising delicious meals during the long Teton winter. They'd canned late into the night last week, laughing about the exploded jar of apple butter and debating whether jalapeño jam really needed that much sugar.

With a grunt, Charlie Grace sank the shovel again and turned another mound of compost. It felt good to work the soil, to mark the end of something with intention. And maybe—if she could admit it to herself—it felt even better to be doing it alone, her thoughts clear.

Suddenly, the distant whine of a saw split the quiet, followed by the rhythmic thud of a nail gun. Charlie Grace winced. The construction crew had returned from their lunch break and were now pounding away at the guest cabins on the east side of the property. What had begun as a promise of growth now grated on her nerves, the constant noise shattering the rare stillness she found in the garden.

She sighed. The peace she'd carved out in the dirt was no match for progress.

The sound of a distant engine rose above the noise of construction, pulling Charlie Grace's attention toward the tree-lined lane that led up from the road. A dust plume curled in the sunlight as a familiar green pickup bounced into view. Lila's truck. Charlie Grace leaned on her shovel, shielding her eyes with one hand and lifting the other in a wave.

Lila parked just off the gravel, boots hitting the ground a second later. She slammed the door with her hip, her long chestnut-colored braid swinging as she made her way over.

"Afternoon," she called, stepping around the wheelbarrow.

"You're just in time for the manure party," Charlie Grace said with a grin.

Lila smirked. "Hard pass."

Charlie Grace gestured toward the porch. "Thanks for coming out to check on the pups."

"Happy to do it," Lila said, swiping her sleeve across her

forehead. "Man, it's still warm out. But frost is coming. You can smell it in the air."

Charlie Grace planted the shovel in the dirt. "Coffee's inside if you want a cup. How's things at Paws in the Pines?" She pointed and started walking in the direction of the house.

Lila groaned, brushing a hand down her jeans as if wiping away the memory. "This morning, we had a Labrador come in with a pus-filled abscess the size of a grapefruit on his—"

Charlie Grace's hands flew up. "Okay! Okay. I take my question back."

Lila laughed, clearly unbothered. "You asked. You know I don't sugarcoat."

"Never have," Charlie Grace muttered, chuckling despite herself. Lila was known for her lack of filters.

Lila shrugged, her face flushed from the afternoon sun—or maybe from the chaos she'd just escaped. "It smelled like roadkill and sour milk, if you must know."

"I mustn't," Charlie Grace said, reaching for the back screen door handle. "But I'm glad you're here. One of the pups seems to be not be eating like the others."

The screen door hinges creaked open as Charlie Grace led the way into the kitchen, the smell of fresh earth trailing in behind them. Sunlight poured through the wide windows, catching the gleam of copper pans hanging over the stove.

Clancy Rivers sat near the window in his wheelchair, a worn copy of a *Western Horseman* magazine propped open in his lap. His reading glasses perched low on his nose, and he looked up with a smile that wrinkled the corners of his eyes.

"Well, look who's come to visit," he said, voice warm and gravelly. "Morning, Lila."

"Hi, Clancy." Lila crossed the kitchen and gave his shoulder a gentle squeeze. "Still keeping Charlie Grace in line?"

"Best I can," he said with a wink. "But she's always been a little headstrong."

"Runs in the family," Charlie Grace said, while washing her hands at the kitchen sink. She brushed her hands on a dish towel, then moved toward the coffee pot.

Clancy nodded toward Lila. "You here to see those dogs Jewel found?"

"Yes," Lila replied, her voice shifting into her vet-clinic tone. "I thought I'd check them over and make sure all's well."

Clancy's brow furrowed. He looked squarely at Charlie Grace. "Don't go letting that little girl get too attached."

Then he turned to Lila. "That granddaughter of mine is just like her mother. She'd adopt a rock if you let her."

Charlie Grace laughed as she poured two mugs. "And mother it by tucking it in each night."

Lila grinned and accepted the coffee. "She's got a soft heart. Nothing wrong with that."

"No, but soft hearts bruise easy," Clancy said, folding his magazine and setting it aside. "Especially when they start thinking every stray was sent just for them."

The comment hung gently in the air, not heavy, just real—and true enough to tug at Charlie Grace's chest. She handed Lila a mug and took a seat beside her dad.

"She's resilient," Charlie Grace said, quieter now. "But I'll keep an eye."

Clancy gave a slight nod, then adjusted his chair with a small humph. "That's all I can hope for, you know. Someone looking out."

He picked up the magazine again but didn't open it, letting the words settle like dust in a sunbeam.

Lila glanced around the kitchen as she took a sip of coffee, her eyes catching the subtle but tasteful changes since her last visit.

"So, what do you think?" Charlie Grace asked, attempting to pry a compliment from her friend.

The old linoleum had been replaced with wide-plank hickory floors, and the cabinets—once a tired, honey oak—were now a creamy white with iron pulls. A new farmhouse sink sat beneath the window, flanked by fresh herbs in terracotta pots. Over the table, a handblown glass light fixture cast soft golden tones across the space. It resembled one she'd seen in a magazine over at Reva's.

"I like what you've done in here," Lila said, turning in place to take it all in. "It still feels like your mama's kitchen, but...lighter somehow."

Clancy snorted from his chair. "Charlie Grace has got a pile of money now and still spends it like it's coming outta my feed budget."

Charlie Grace's lips twitched, but she didn't look at him right away. She kept her gaze on the sink for a moment longer, then offered a careful smile—one that didn't quite reach her eyes.

"I'm just trying to be thoughtful about expenditures," she said quietly, the rim of her coffee mug pressed to her lips. "Money doesn't change everything."

Clancy let out a soft grunt, more sentiment than sass, and looked away.

Lila glanced between them but said nothing. She set her mug down, fingers tracing the rim absently. "Reva left town early this morning."

Charlie Grace scowled. "Left? What do you mean?"

"Her Grand Memaw's not doing well," Lila said gently. "She got the call yesterday afternoon. Packed a bag and caught the first flight to Atlanta."

Clancy looked up from his magazine. "That old woman still hanging on? Lord, I remember Reva talking about her back when you girls were in pigtails."

"She's been the backbone of that family," Lila said. "And from what Reva told me, she's slipping fast. Her mama said it's a matter of days, maybe less."

Charlie Grace's eyes softened. "Poor Reva. She's always been so close to her Grand Memaw. Remember how she used to send those care packages to her every holiday, and sometimes for no reason at all? Pecan pralines and cans of boiled peanuts?"

Lila smiled faintly. "And handwritten notes with Bible verses underlined in red ink. Reva used to roll her eyes, but you could tell she kept every single one."

Clancy shifted in his chair. "That woman raised Reva right. Gave her a strong spine and a good heart. You don't see that much anymore."

"She's got all of that and more," Charlie Grace said. "But still—this will be hard. I know how much she hates leaving Thunder Mountain. Even just for a few days."

Lila leaned back, folding her arms. "Not to mention Kellen and Lucan. Even so, this is not just a visit. Her mom hinted that there may be decisions ahead—big ones. The family's pecan farm is a lot to manage. Her daddy's not getting any younger. The boys can't seem to manage things on their own anymore. Reva's going to feel that pull."

A long silence fell over the kitchen. The ticking of the wall clock and the muffled hum of construction outside filled the space between them.

Charlie Grace finally spoke, her voice tight. "What are you saying?"

Lila didn't answer right away. "Nothing particular. But Reva's never been the type to walk away from responsibility. If her family needs her...I don't know. She might try to find a way to do both, but something's gotta give."

Clancy tapped a finger on the armrest of his wheelchair.

"That girl's got a sense of duty a mile wide. Always did. Even as a teenager, she was looking after everyone else."

"Still is," Charlie Grace murmured. Her mind was already tumbling through what Reva's absence would mean—even if part-time—for the town, for their group, for the quiet rhythm they'd all come to rely on. "Well, we all know she'll die trying to do it all."

Lila nodded. "And without letting anyone know she's breaking a sweat."

A sudden thumping overhead broke the quiet moment, followed by the hurried patter of small feet on the stairs. Jewel burst into the kitchen, her cheeks flushed and eyes bright with purpose. In her arms she cradled a bundle of fabric—scraps trailing like streamers, edges frayed where they'd been hastily cut.

Charlie Grace turned at the noise, eyebrows lifting. "What in the world—?"

Jewel held out the bundle proudly. "I brought blankets for the puppies!"

Lila leaned forward to get a better look, her smile forming before she could stop it.

Charlie Grace's brow furrowed as she reached out and fingered one of the strips. Her face fell. "Young lady...these are my good towels."

Jewel blinked. "But the puppies need blankets."

"They need something warm, not Egyptian cotton," Charlie Grace said, half amused, half exasperated. She held up one of the tattered pieces. "These were wedding gifts."

Jewel looked genuinely puzzled. "You're not even married anymore."

Lila snorted into her coffee.

Clancy chuckled. "She's got you there, honey."

Charlie Grace shot him a look but couldn't keep the grin off her face. "That's not the point. We have plenty of old towels in the utility closet. Why didn't you ask first?"

Jewel hugged the scraps closer to her chest. "Because the puppies were shivering, and I didn't want to waste time."

Lila leaned back, watching the exchange with quiet admiration. "She's got her priorities straight."

Charlie Grace sighed, her hands falling to her hips. "She'd give away the whole house if it meant keeping those pups comfortable."

Clancy nodded toward Lila. "Didn't I tell you? Just like her mama."

Charlie Grace laughed again, shaking her head. "Enough out of you."

Jewel's eyes sparkled as she turned, already heading for the door. "I'll be in the barn!"

As the door banged shut behind her, Lila stood and stretched. "Well, I guess that's my cue."

Charlie Grace followed her to the door, pausing to grab a basket of supplies she'd gathered earlier. "Come on. Let's go see if those rocks my daughter adopted have started barking."

The sun filtered through the trees as Charlie Grace and Lila made their way down the worn path toward the barn, the crunch of gravel beneath their boots mingling with the distant hum of a saw from the guest cabins.

Charlie Grace shifted the basket of clean rags and ointments to her other hip. "So... how's Camille doing? She must be getting close now."

Lila exhaled a soft laugh, shaking her head. "Seven months. Can you believe it? She's finally slowed down enough to let me fuss over her, which is saying something. Last week she tried to reorganize her entire closet at the house, then had a Braxton Hicks scare and promised she'd sit still for at least a day."

Charlie Grace smirked. "Sounds familiar. Like mother, like daughter."

"She's definitely got my stubborn streak," Lila admitted. "But she's good. Really good. Her cheeks are all rosy, and she gets winded climbing stairs, but she's eating well, reading all the baby books I never finished, and she's obsessed with figuring out the best kind of cloth diapers."

Charlie Grace laughed. "Cloth diapers? Lord help her."

"I know," Lila said, grinning. "She's convinced it's better for the environment. She's also convinced she can get by without sleep, coffee, or help, which—spoiler alert—she cannot."

"Does she know yet if it's a boy or a girl?"

"Nope. She wants to be surprised," Lila said, glancing sideways. "Though if you ask me, that nursery's looking suspiciously gender-neutral in a way that leans toward baby boy. Lots of sage green and navy."

Charlie Grace nodded with a soft smile. "She seems more settled than I expected."

"She is," Lila said, her voice gentling. "Hard as it was, it's like she's made her peace with what's coming—and she's proud of herself. I am, too."

They reached the barn doors just as Jewel popped her head out, a smear of something suspiciously muddy on her cheek. "They're ready!"

Charlie Grace opened the door with a knowing look. "Brace yourself," she murmured to Lila. "You're walking into full-blown puppy love."

Lila chuckled. "Aren't I always?"

Inside the barn, dust motes floated lazily in the sunbeams slanting through the opening. In the far stall, Jewel knelt in the straw, the cut-up towel pieces now arranged like patchwork bedding around the cluster of pups.

"They're sleeping," she whispered, holding a finger to her lips.

Lila crouched beside her, pulling latex gloves from her back pocket and slipping them on with a snap. "Let's take a look anyway, sweetheart. I won't wake them more than I have to."

Charlie Grace leaned against the stall door, folding her arms and watching with quiet interest as Lila worked. The pups were nestled close, a pile of fuzzy limbs and twitching noses. Six in total—some dark, some pale, all with thick, plush coats and broad little paws.

Lila reached gently for the nearest one, lifting it with practiced care. She examined its ears, eyes, and belly, then ran her fingers down each limb with precision. Her brow creased.

She set the pup down and picked up another. Then another.

Charlie Grace straightened. "Something wrong?"

Lila didn't answer right away. She was focused, her eyes sharp now in a way that made Charlie Grace's stomach flutter.

Jewel looked up nervously. "Are they okay?"

"They seem healthy," Lila said slowly, keeping her voice calm. "Good muscle tone. Clear eyes. Eating well, I assume?"

"Like little pigs," Charlie Grace confirmed. "We've been bottle-feeding every four hours. They gobble it down. Well, except for the tiniest one." She pointed. "But she's doing a little better."

Lila lifted the last pup and examined the pads of its feet, then gently turned it on its back. Her fingers hovered over its growing canines, then moved to the fur around its ruff.

Charlie Grace stepped into the stall. "Lila?"

Lila sat back on her heels and slowly peeled off her gloves. Her eyes met Charlie Grace's, serious now. "They're not dogs."

Charlie Grace blinked. "What do you mean they're not dogs?"

"They *look* like dogs," Lila repeated, nodding. "But I'm ninety percent sure these are wolf pups."

Charlie Grace gasped. "Wolves?"

Lila softened her tone as she turned to Jewel. "Sweetheart,

they're not dangerous right now. But they're wild animals. They don't grow up to be pets—not the way dogs do."

Charlie Grace felt a chill prickle her skin. "You sure?"

"I'll need to run some DNA to confirm, but the markers are there. The paws, the length of the snout, the shape of the ears—too narrow, too pointed. And the way their coats are coming in? That thick, layered underfur? It's classic."

Jewel's lower lip trembled. "But I've been singing to them. They know my voice. They wag their tails!"

"I know, baby," Charlie Grace said softly, wrapping an arm around her daughter's shoulders. "Let's just hear what Lila thinks we should do next."

Lila looked between them, her face full of compassion. "We'll take this one step at a time. First, I'll get the DNA testing done. Then we'll figure out next steps—together. But I want to prepare you both...if they are wolves, there'll be regulations. This may be out of our hands."

Charlie Grace met Lila's gaze, heart sinking. She looked down at the sleeping pups, nestled so trustingly against each other in the straw. Jewel had called them hers. Had already given them names.

If Lila was right, her daughter's world was about to shift. This wasn't just a passing cloud—they were on the leading edge of an emotional storm. And they'd just felt the first drop.

7

Capri stood at the front door, twisting the lid onto the thermos as coffee-scented steam curled into the cool morning air. She held it out, and Jake took it from her with one hand, the other settling on her waist as he leaned in and kissed her, his whiskers grazing her skin in that way she secretly loved.

He wore worn jeans that clung just right, a thick leather tool belt slung low around his hips, and a navy ball cap pulled down to shade his eyes from the early morning glare. He looked every inch the man who could rebuild her life.

"Dubois is almost three hours each way," he said, adjusting the strap on his shoulder bag. "Might not be back till dark."

She nodded, fighting the tug in her chest. "Drive safe."

He paused on the porch, one hand on the railing. "Capri...think about what we talked about last night."

Her stomach fluttered at the mention of it. The wedding. She'd brushed him off with a joke, but they both knew it wasn't nothing.

"I will," she promised softly.

When he looked skeptical, she quickly reassured him. "I will think about it."

He nodded once, then strode down the steps and across the gravel drive, boots crunching. She stayed in the doorway until the truck disappeared beyond the pines.

With a sigh, she closed the door and padded barefoot into the kitchen. The chill of the tile floor seeped through her skin as she poured herself a mug of coffee from the pot Jake had set to brew before sunrise. She wrapped both hands around the cup and leaned her hip against the counter.

I'll think about it.

Her eyes drifted toward the window and the view beyond where a soft mist still hung low over the fields. The truth was, there wasn't a good reason to wait. No cold feet, no lingering doubts—just a stubborn little voice inside her that didn't like being rushed. But he hadn't pushed. Not really. Jake never did. He just planted seeds and waited for her to let them bloom.

She didn't want a fuss. That much was certain. No bridesmaids, no color scheme, no tissue paper invitations. If it were up to her—and it was—Pastor Pete would marry them in the wildflower meadow behind Moose Chapel. Reva, Lila and Charlie Grace would be there. That's it. Especially since Jake's family had already declined to travel from Arkansas. Instead, she and Jake planned a trip for Thanksgiving so Capri could meet them.

Capri took a sip of coffee and smiled faintly to herself. Simple. Intimate. Just right.

Still, people would want to celebrate. And she supposed it wouldn't kill her to let them. A gathering at the Rustic Pine afterward. Low-key. Laughter. Toes tapping to Annie's old jukebox in the corner. That would be enough.

Her thoughts settled into a warm stillness, the kind that whispered of something right around the corner. She set her mug down and pushed away from the counter.

Time to see if it still existed.

In the hallway, she reached for the attic pull-down. The rope was stiff with age, and it took two tries to tug the stairs down. They creaked in protest as she climbed, her left leg trembling by the third rung. The injuries from the avalanche still whispered warnings now and then, but she ignored them. Grit carried her up the last steps. That and some careful maneuvering.

The attic was dim and dust-laced, the scent of old cedar and forgotten memories thick in the air. Morning light filtered through a single cobwebbed window, casting long shadows over stacks of boxes, rusted lamp bases, and an unplugged lava lamp. Her mom's holiday wreaths leaned against a busted rocking horse. A crate of old vinyl records sat half open, and the corner of a macramé wall hanging peeked from a box labeled *For Donation*.

Capri stepped carefully between a broken laundry basket and a suitcase missing its handle. She found the trunk tucked beneath an old chenille bedspread. Heart thudding, she flipped the latches and eased it open.

Inside, neatly folded, was a zipped-up wardrobe bag.

She took it with both hands and made her way back down the attic stairs slowly, carefully—each step deliberate. At the bottom, she caught her breath, then walked into the bedroom.

The room was cozy and unpretentious, with cotton curtains hung at the window and a worn quilt draped over the bed—one her mother had stitched years ago, its pattern soft from countless washes. A small dresser held a cluster of wildflowers in a mason jar, and the faint scent of lavender lingered in the air.

She laid the garment bag across her quilt and slowly unzipped it.

There it was.

White eyelet cotton with delicate ribbon piping in soft

yellow. Little matching buttons ran down the bodice, stopping at the waist where the skirt flared just enough. Thin straps. A sweetheart neckline. Classic 1970s prairie style—Gunne Sax. Vintage perfection.

A grin tugged at her mouth as her fingers skimmed the fabric. Her mom's dress. The one she'd admired since girlhood, hanging in the back of the closet, smelling faintly of lavender sachets and possibility.

Too bad her mom and Earl Dunlop were off-grid somewhere in the Salmon River Mountains of central Idaho, trying to out-fish each other with no bars of cell service between them. Not that Capri was certain her mother would come to the wedding anyway.

Still, she'd send a text. Just to say she was invited.

Capri stepped into the dress and zipped it up with a little maneuvering. She padded to the mirror and studied herself— barefoot, no makeup, hair still mussed from sleep. But the dress...

It fit.

She smoothed her hands down the skirt, her reflection nodding back at her, calm and certain.

Yup...it was time to get married.

8

The crush of humanity inside Atlanta's Hartsfield-Jackson airport always made Reva feel like she was in the middle of a marching band parade—minus the music and charm. She navigated through the terminal in stilettos that clicked too loud on the tile, her roller bag nipping at her heels like an impatient toddler.

Outside, the thick Southern air hit her like a slap, clinging to her skin and puffing up her hair within seconds. Lord have mercy, she didn't miss this part. The Wyoming mountains had their quirks—blizzards, wild bears, earthquakes of late—but at least you could breathe without feeling like you were being smothered in a damp quilt.

She picked up the rental car, a nondescript sedan that smelled like air freshener and old coffee, and merged onto the freeway, the skyline rising ahead like a glittering wall of steel and glass. Traffic thickened, a familiar snarl of brake lights and honking. As she eased into the chaos, her thoughts tangled with emotion. She wasn't just heading to see her sick Grand Memaw. She was heading home—and that word had never felt so complicated.

The hospital lobby was a swirl of artificial calm—floor-to-ceiling windows tried to let in light, but the overhead fluorescents fought back. Potted plants stood like sentries in the corners, and the air smelled of antiseptic and overworked HVAC. Nurses bustled past with clipboards and coffee cups. A television mounted on the wall broadcast a muted talk show no one was watching.

Reva stepped up to the front desk, smoothing her blouse, suddenly wishing she'd thought to reapply her lipstick. "Hi, could you tell me which room Rosetta Nygard is in?"

Before the young woman behind the counter could respond, a voice behind her wrapped around Reva like a velvet ribbon.

"There you are."

Reva turned.

Her mother, Nadine Nygard, swept through the automatic doors like royalty returning to court. Her stride was graceful but determined, her spine arrow straight. She wore a navy sheath dress with pearl buttons, cream heels that never seemed to scuff, and a coordinating pillbox hat perched just so atop her meticulously pressed black curls. A faint whiff of gardenia trailed in her wake, and she carried a monogrammed leather handbag that had likely cost more than Reva's first car.

Her makeup was flawless, of course—lipstick precisely drawn, lashes lifted, brows arched like question marks. But her eyes—those deep, mahogany eyes Reva had inherited—were lined with fatigue and something heavier beneath.

Her mama gathered her into a light, ladylike hug that smelled of home. "Ree-Ree, you finally made it."

Reva held onto the hug a beat longer than she meant to. Her mother's embrace had always been more composed than comforting—more about appearances than affection—but today, it felt different. Tighter. Real.

"She's been askin' for you," her mama said softly, pulling

back but keeping a hand on Reva's arm as if grounding them both.

"How is she?" Reva asked, her voice catching before she could steady it.

Her mama's expression faltered for the briefest moment, then firmed. "Stubborn as ever. But tired. She's been holding court in that room like it's her parlor. Still wants her lipstick, still critiques the nurses like they're contestants in a pageant." A ghost of a smile lifted the corners of her mouth. "But it's... different now. She's not bouncing back like she used to. She had a horrible episode. The doctors are saying it's her heart. I suppose at age ninety-two, it's just getting tired and giving out."

Reva nodded, throat tight. "I should've come sooner."

"Baby, you came when it mattered," her mama said, pressing a hand to her cheek. "Now come on. Let's get you upstairs. They're all waiting."

They stepped into the elevator, the doors closing with a quiet whoosh. Reva watched the numbers light up above the door as they ascended, her reflection in the brushed metal warped and tired. She tugged at the hems of her sleeves, suddenly self-conscious in her travel-wrinkled blouse.

The elevator dinged on the third floor, and they stepped into a hallway lined with cheerful art and bulletin boards announcing flu shots and prayer meetings. The hum of machines and muffled voices drifted from the rooms, punctuated by the occasional nurse's laugh or the beeping of a monitor.

Outside room 312, her brother Quincy stood, tall and broad-shouldered in a dress shirt with the sleeves rolled up. His tie hung loose around his neck like he'd tried to look presentable and gave up halfway through. Next to him, Scarlett, his wife, clutched a quilted purse and offered a weak smile when she saw Reva.

"There she is," Quincy said, his voice rough as he pulled

Reva into a one-armed hug that felt both strong and sagging with fatigue.

Her older brother, Mason, nodded. "Memaw's been askin' for you every ten minutes. You'd think we were chopped liver."

Scarlett reached for Reva's hand. "We're so glad you're here. It means a lot to her. To all of us."

Reva swallowed hard, heart pounding in her chest like a drumbeat she couldn't slow. Behind the door, the woman who raised them all—who made sweet tea strong enough to cure anything and never let a soul leave her house hungry—was waiting.

Her mama stepped forward, smoothing the front of her dress. "Let's go on in. But fair warning—despite her frailty, she's in rare form. Told the doctor this morning she didn't care for his handshake."

Reva smiled faintly, her nerves settling into something else. Something like reverence.

The door creaked softly as Reva stepped into the hospital room.

The blinds had been drawn to soften the harsh light, and a bouquet of fresh flowers—garden roses and lilies, likely brought by Scarlett—sat in a glass vase near the window. The scent didn't quite cover the underlying sterility of antiseptic and plastic tubing. A television murmured quietly in the corner, tuned to a game show Grand Memaw would've normally hollered answers at. But not today.

Reva's breath caught in her throat.

Rosetta Nygard, the indomitable matriarch of the family, looked impossibly small against the starch-white hospital sheets. Her skin had thinned to parchment, stretched loosely over fragile bones. Her once-luxurious gray hair—always curled and coiffed—lay flat against the pillow, like cotton left in the rain. A nasal cannula fed oxygen to her with soft hissing breaths, and her hands, those same hands that had stirred cornbread batter and snapped green beans by the bushel, now trembled as they rested against her quilted lap blanket.

But her eyes—still a sharp, soulful brown—lit up when they found Reva.

"Well, would you look what the wind blew in," Grand Memaw said, her voice surprisingly steady, though her lips moved slowly, like every syllable had to be coaxed out of her. "My girl from the mountains."

Reva stepped closer, trying not to betray her shock. She leaned down, kissing her grandmother's cheek, which felt too warm and too thin all at once. "Hey, Memaw."

"Mmm," the old woman murmured, her eyes drifting to the others who'd followed Reva into the room. "I got just enough left in me for one more private talk."

Reva's mama raised a brow. "Grand Memaw, don't go stirrin' up emotions. Ree-Ree just got here."

"I ain't stirrin' nothin' but my soul, child," Grand Memaw said, waving a frail hand toward the door. "Now hush and give us a minute. Quincy, Scarlett—you too. I love y'all, but I need to talk to my Reva."

Her voice, once like a church bell ringing over a Sunday picnic, began to thin—trailing off like smoke from an evening fire. Reva could almost hear it slipping away with the next breath.

Reva's mama hesitated, smoothing a crease in her skirt before nodding at her daughter. "We'll be just outside. Don't wear her out."

When the door closed behind them, the room felt suddenly hushed. As if time had paused, just for the two of them.

Reva pulled the nearby chair close and took Grand Memaw's hand, careful not to press too hard. "I'm here, Memaw. I'm right here."

Her grandmother's eyes glistened, but her mouth curled faintly with a private smile.

"I know you are," she whispered, her voice barely more than a thread now. "That's why I waited."

Grand Memaw's breath rattled slightly as she adjusted her head on the pillow. Her hand, soft as linen but shaking now, reached for Reva's and didn't let go.

"I reckon it won't be long now," she murmured, eyes fixed on something past the ceiling, as if she could already see beyond it. "Your granddaddy's been gone near twenty years. Your daddy, too. And I feel them callin' me home."

Reva blinked back tears, her throat tight.

"But before I go," Grand Memaw whispered, her voice barely more than a hush of wind across cotton fields. "There are things I need to settle."

She turned her gaze to Reva, and suddenly, her grip tightened with surprising strength. "Sunnyside Acres."

Reva's heart stilled.

Grand Memaw's eyes shone—clear, urgent. "That land... it ain't just soil and trees. It's blood. My daddy—your great-granddaddy, Jeremiah Shelby—he carved it out with his own two hands. Just a boy when freedom came. No shoes, no money, not even a last name. He got to choose. But he worked. First for sharecroppers, then for himself. Bought forty acres from a white man who thought the soil was too poor to grow anything worthwhile. But your great-granddaddy saw promise."

She paused, catching her breath. Reva leaned in, letting the words soak through her like gospel.

"Pecans don't come easy," Grand Memaw went on, her voice growing raspy. "Takes patience. Years 'fore a tree yields anything worth shellin'. But Jeremiah planted anyway. Said he was planting for grandchildren he hadn't met yet. Said we had to make something that would outlive us."

Her lips trembled, then firmed.

"I watched my daddy build that farm. Watched your daddy

sweat on that land, sunup to sundown, never complainin'. And I kept it goin' long as I could."

Tears slid silently down Reva's cheeks.

"I heard Quincy talkin' to that real estate man," Grand Memaw said, her voice breaking now. "He's gon' sell it. Turn it into vacation rentals or—Lord knows what." She shook her head, eyes burning. "He don't see it the way we do."

She squeezed Reva's hand again, more fiercely this time.

"You do. I know you do. That land remembers who we are. It made us who we are."

Reva opened her mouth, but no words came.

"I need you to come home," Grand Memaw whispered, as her voice dimmed. "Run Sunnyside. Keep the legacy alive. For me."

Reva sat frozen, the weight of generations settling across her shoulders, heavy and unrelenting.

She had a life in Thunder Mountain. A job. A husband. A son. And...friends.

But this...this was her bloodline asking for one final promise.

Reva sat still, Grand Memaw's frail fingers wrapped tight around hers, as the words echoed in the quiet room.

Come home. Run Sunnyside. For me.

Her thoughts flitted unbidden to Thunder Mountain—Kellen's strong hands fixing breakfast on sleepy Saturday mornings, the way Lucan's laughter filled every empty space in their home. Her precious boy. She pictured him scampering through the orchards at Sunnyside, his small hands stretching toward branches bowed with pecans—darting between trees planted by men he'd never meet, but whose sweat still lingered in the soil, their labor a quiet gift to his future.

Her sweet boy, full of light and promise, raised by love and the roots of something deeper than time. Lucan hadn't come to them by birth, but by divine design—placed in their arms through grace, not chance.

Maybe it wasn't just about honoring the past. Maybe it was about securing the future. Lucan's future.

Yes, it would be a sacrifice. But how much had this old woman sacrificed for her family?

How could she possibly turn down Grand Memaw's request? A family legacy meant something—didn't it?

She looked down at their joined hands—her own steady and strong, her grandmother's fragile, trembling like the last autumn leaf hanging on a branch.

Reva bent closer, her voice barely more than a breath.

"Yes," she whispered against the tightness in her throat. "Don't worry. I'll come home."

Grand Memaw exhaled, a slow, shivering sound that seemed to carry a lifetime of relief.

And for the first time since Reva had stepped into the room, the old woman smiled with her whole face.

9

"I hate you!"

The words hit harder than they should have as Jewel spun on her heel and dashed up the stairs, the slap of her socked feet echoing off the walls. A moment later, her bedroom door slammed with enough force to rattle the old photographs hanging in the hallway.

Charlie Grace winced. Motherhood certainly wasn't for the faint of heart.

She took a steadying breath, her hand still curled around the back of a kitchen chair.

Lila had called it yesterday. Wolves. Not dogs.

Charlie Grace had spent most of the night tossing and turning, the weight of that revelation pressing down on her chest. She'd made the call to the Fish and Game Department first thing that morning. Now they were on their way to pick up the pups.

"Timing's everything," Lila had said when she prepared to leave yesterday. "They're still young enough to be rehabilitated. But the longer they're with humans..."

Charlie Grace had nodded, even as her heart cracked just thinking about her daughter's tear-streaked face.

A soft knock on the front door pulled her back to the present.

"Must be them," her dad remarked, still gazing up the stairs where his granddaughter was hiding.

She nodded and opened the door to find two uniformed wildlife officers standing beside Lila, who offered a sad smile.

"Morning, Ms. Rivers," one of the officers said. "I'm Officer Grant. This is my partner, Officer Hernandez."

Charlie Grace grabbed her jacket. "Let me show you to the pups. They're in the barn."

Lila gave her arm a reassuring squeeze as they passed. "You're doing the right thing."

Charlie Grace swallowed hard and motioned for the officers to follow.

Officer Grant adjusted his cap against the morning sun. "Pretty place you've got here."

Charlie Grace gave a nod, arms crossed against the chill. "Thank you. It's been in the family a long time."

Officer Hernandez glanced toward the distant tree line. "That where your daughter found them?"

Charlie pointed with her chin. "Just beyond that fence line, near the creek. She and my Aunt Mo thought they were abandoned. Brought them home."

Grant gave a small, understanding smile. "Happens more than you'd think. Most folks don't have a vet friend on hand to break the news. They discover much later when the pups start acting more wild than domestic—and by then, it's a whole lot harder to undo. We've seen cases where they get aggressive, start hunting livestock, or even bite people. That's when the calls come in, and sadly, it doesn't always end well for the animal."

Charlie managed a small laugh. "Lila didn't sugarcoat anything; I'll give her that."

Hernandez chuckled. "She never does."

They reached the barn. Charlie paused at the door. "My daughter is up in her room. Heartbroken."

Grant's tone softened. "We'll keep that in mind."

Inside, the pups stirred in the crate, one of them letting out a high-pitched whimper. The others were huddled together in the worn quilt Jewel had insisted on using, their tiny sides rising and falling in rhythm.

The officers knelt beside the crate, inspecting the pups with gentle hands and quiet voices. Officer Grant glanced at Lila. "So, these are the six? All taken in within the last four days?"

Lila nodded. "Yes. The pups were kept here in the barn."

Charlie Grace stepped forward. "We honestly thought they were just...lost puppies. Jewel made a little nest back by the grain bags. She's been feeding them and sleeping beside them every night."

"She's eight?" Hernandez asked, eyes softening.

Charlie Grace nodded. "And she's taking all this very hard."

Grant stood and removed a small tablet from his vest. "I'll need to take a brief statement. Just confirming what Lila told us."

Charlie Grace recounted everything—how Jewel had found them, how they looked like strays, the vet check, the realization they were wolves. As she spoke, the officers listened carefully, never making her feel blamed or foolish.

"Well, that should do it," Grant said, clicking off the screen. "You did right by calling us. Most folks don't."

Hernandez reached for the crate. "We'll load them carefully and get them to the Jackson rehab center."

Charlie Grace watched as the officers lifted the crate and carried it out. Lila and Charlie Grace trailed behind.

They set the crate down, and Officer Hernandez pulled a large set of keys from her pants pocket.

Charlie Grace's gaze drifted upward, past the crate and toward the upstairs window of the house. A pale curtain fluttered slightly.

She blinked. Then looked again.

Jewel's small face was barely visible behind the lace curtain, eyes wide, mouth drawn tight.

"Wait," Charlie Grace said, holding up a hand. "Can you give me a minute?"

Officer Grant nodded. "Of course."

She raced inside and took the stairs two at a time, pausing just outside her daughter's door. Her knuckles hovered above the wood.

"Jewel," she said softly, "it's me."

No answer.

Charlie Grace eased the door open.

Jewel sat curled on the window seat, knees hugged to her chest, face blotchy from crying.

"They're leaving," her daughter whispered.

Charlie Grace walked over and sat beside her. "I know, baby. But they're going where they belong. People who can help them learn to live in the wild again."

Jewel's voice cracked. "But they need me."

Charlie Grace wrapped an arm around her shoulders. "They needed you to keep them safe until the right people could take over. And you did that, sweetie. You did an amazing job."

Jewel didn't move.

"The pups are downstairs," Charlie Grace said gently. "Still in their crate. Would you come say goodbye?"

Jewel looked at her with a fresh rush of tears.

Charlie Grace smiled. "C'mon, puddin'. Come say goodbye."

She stood and offered her hand. After a long pause, Jewel took it.

They walked down the stairs slowly, hand in hand. When they stepped out into the yard, the officers turned with warm expressions.

"Is this the young lady who found them?" Grant asked.

Jewel gave a shy nod, eyes fixed on the crate.

Officer Hernandez knelt and unfastened a pouch on her vest. "You know," she said, "we've worked with a lot of people over the years, but not everyone has the heart and courage to do what you did."

Jewel glanced up, surprised.

"You helped save six lives," Hernandez added. "And that makes you something pretty special."

She held out a small bronze pin shaped like a paw print with a star in the center. The engraving read *Junior Wildlife Officer.*

Jewel's mouth parted as she reached out and took it with both hands.

"We don't give these out often," Grant added with a wink. "But we think you've more than earned it."

Jewel's face lit up. "I'm one of you now?"

"You sure are," Hernandez said. "And if you ever want to come see how the pups are doing prior to when they're turned out into the wild, we'll make it happen."

Charlie Grace watched as Jewel knelt beside the crate and whispered her goodbyes to each pup. There were no more tears —just a quiet sense of understanding. Of pride.

The officers eased the crate into the back of the waiting truck, their movements slow and respectful. Charlie Grace stood with her daughter beside her, the breeze lifting Jewel's hair as she clutched the pin to her chest.

Yes—motherhood wasn't for the faint of heart. It didn't require grand gestures.

Sometimes, it was simply standing shoulder to shoulder with a little girl who was trying to be brave.

10

Reva squinted through the airplane window as the familiar outline of the Tetons came into view, jagged and proud, their snowy peaks lit by the early evening sun. As the plane dipped lower toward the Jackson Hole airport, a tightness wrapped around her ribs—part homesickness, part dread.

This was home. She'd only been gone a week, and it felt like a month.

And yet...her heart was still back in Georgia, wrapped in hospital sheets and a grandmother's failing breath.

The wheels touched down with a soft screech, and the plane slowed to a crawl on the runway. Reva barely noticed the bustle of passengers rising, collecting bags and exchanging polite smiles. She moved on autopilot, her mind crowded with questions she hadn't dared answer.

Inside the terminal, the crowd parted—and there they were.

Lucan broke free from Kellen's grasp, his little legs pumping. "Mama!"

Reva dropped her bag and scooped him up, burying her

face in his curls, breathing him in like a woman starved. Kellen caught up, his expression equal parts relief and concern.

"You okay?" he asked, brushing her hair from her face.

She nodded, swallowing back the lump that had lodged there since Atlanta. "Thanks for retrieving my car and then coming back to pick me up. Let's get out of here."

They made it to the car without much conversation, Lucan already chattering in the back seat. "Mama, I found a rock that looks like a potato. It's in my pocket—wait, no...it was in my pocket."

Reva smiled, but it didn't reach her eyes.

As they pulled onto the highway, Kellen glanced at her. "So...how was it? How's Grand Memaw?"

Reva exhaled slowly, turning toward the window. "Not good. Worse than I've ever seen her. She's skin and bones now, but still stubborn as ever. One minute she's making perfect sense, the next she's falling asleep mid-sentence."

Kellen didn't say anything, just reached for her hand.

Reva continued, her voice quieter now. "Mama's already talking about the funeral—where to hold it, who to call, what kind of hat she'll wear. She means well, but she's steeped in social expectations. Always has been. Her world runs on handwritten thank-you notes, heirloom linens, and the quiet currency of reputation."

"And your brother?" Kellen asked. "Is he helping?"

Reva hesitated. "Quincy's fine. He and Scarlett haven't changed much. But...he made a comment that stuck with me. Said something about 'waiting on the loan paperwork to come through,' but then he changed the subject real quick. When I pressed him, he finally admitted he's buying a Cirrus SR22."

Kellen's eyebrows lifted. "An airplane?"

"Apparently a very nice one."

"Yeah, those planes can run a half mil, new."

Reva nodded. "Seems like an outrageous splurge to me. He's

usually better with money than that. It's probably nothing, but...I don't know. Something felt off." She didn't mention that he was seeking to sell the pecan farm.

Kellen pulled onto Highway 26 and headed north. "Sounds like you've got a lot on your mind."

She turned to face him fully then, her voice steady. "I do."

A beat of silence passed. And then—quietly, deliberately—Reva said the words she'd been holding since she left Georgia.

"I think I need to go back. For good."

Kellen's jaw tightened slightly. He didn't look at her, but the air in the car seemed to shift. Even Lucan, humming to himself in the back, grew suddenly quiet.

Reva stared out the windshield, heart pounding, waiting for her husband to say something.

Anything.

Kellen kept his eyes on the road, the lines blurring past in the headlights. One hand stayed on the wheel, the other still loosely holding hers, though she could feel the tension in his fingers now.

"You mean...move to Georgia?" he said at last, as if testing how the words tasted in his mouth. "Like—*move* move?"

Reva nodded, barely. "She asked me to take over Sunnyside Acres. Said it was my calling. Said she didn't want it to leave the family."

"What about your brother?" Kellen posed, asking the obvious.

"She says he's already talking to realtors. That, coupled with the spending—well, leaving Sunnyside solely in his control might end badly. And before you ask if I could run the pecan operation from here, the answer is not likely. I'm good at a lot of things, but juggling crop yields, irrigation schedules, and payroll from two thousand miles away isn't one of them."

She paused, her voice quieter now.

"Truth is, I'm already spread too thin. Between mayoral

duties, casework piling up at the firm, and trying to be a good mama to Lucan...something's always slipping through the cracks. I already lie awake most nights wondering which one of those balls will hit the ground first."

She looked at Kellen then, her eyes shining. "But the farm in Georgia—it's more than just dirt and trees. It's my family's legacy."

A long pause. Lucan, behind them, had gone quiet, lulled by the motion of the car or maybe sensing the shift in his parents' voices.

Kellen exhaled through his nose, slow and deliberate. "I figured something was weighing on you. Just didn't expect...this."

"I didn't either." Her voice cracked slightly. "My great-granddaddy started with nothing but callused hands and the will to build something that would last. He carved Sunnyside Acres from red clay and grit, in a time when the world gave him every reason to fail. But he didn't He held on. And so did the generations after him. This is Lucan's heritage."

He nodded again, but slower this time. "I get that. I really do, Reva. But what about us? Our life here. Our work. Your mayor's seat. This is our home. What you're talking about—well, it's big. You know?"

She didn't answer. Not right away.

Kellen glanced at her, then back to the road, his voice gentler now. "I'm not saying no. I'm just saying...this isn't small. There are a lot of consequences to consider."

The tires hummed against the pavement, filling the silence between them.

Reva stared out into the dusk. "Believe me, I know."

11

Reva pushed open the door to City Hall, her heels clicking across the polished tile. She wasn't three steps into the foyer before Verna appeared like a prairie dog out of a burrow, lips tight and bun tighter. "You're back," she said, as if Reva might've returned from a vacation rather than a week of emotional upheaval and family wrangling. "I've made a list."

Of course, she had.

Reva adjusted the strap of her leather tote, already sensing the inbox overload awaiting her upstairs. "Good morning to you, too, Verna."

Verna handed over a clipboard so thick it should've come with an arm brace. "First, the building permits backlog. Then the community center roof leaked—again. And the Rocky Mountain Oyster festival committee is demanding you pick a date before Friday's planning meeting. But most urgent—" she lowered her voice, glancing toward the stairwell. "Fleet Southcott forgot his cruiser keys. Again. Except this time, he left them in the ignition. Engine running. All night."

Reva winced. "Tell me someone found it before the car ran out of gas."

"They found it alright. Idling in front of the bakery. Sheriff Southcott apparently went in for a cinnamon roll and forgot both the car and the time. Stood there thirty minutes chatting with Boyd before he took off and walked home, leaving the car behind."

Reva closed her eyes for a beat. Thunder Mountain's beloved sheriff had served the town for decades. But lately… there had been signs. Misplacing his citation book. Wandering into the Knit Wit gatherings at the Rustic Pine thinking it was poker night. Reva had chalked it up to age and fatigue. But now?

"Add a meeting with Fleet to the list," she said, eyes opening again with resolve.

"I already did," Verna said, straightening. "Three o'clock. His wife promised to call him with a reminder to make sure he wouldn't forget."

Reva climbed the stairs, clipboard in hand, the weight of it all settling into her shoulders. As much as she wanted to slide gently back into the rhythm of being mayor of Thunder Mountain, the job—and this town—rarely waited for anyone.

She stepped into her office and shut the door with a soft click, muffling the hum of the municipal building behind her, then dropped her tote and the clipboard onto the wide walnut desk and stood still for a moment, eyes sweeping over the room she'd made her own.

The walls were lined with local artwork—photos of the Tetons in every season, a woven tapestry from a Shoshone artisan, a framed thank-you card drawn in crayon from Lucan's Sunday school class.

Warm mountain light streamed in through the tall windows, brushing across her leather chair, the fresh vase of daisies Verna must've set out, and the carefully stacked files waiting in her inbox like silent sentinels.

This was home. Her domain. Her calling.

And soon...it wouldn't be.

She sank into the chair and exhaled, staring out the window at the fluttering aspen leaves, a few at the top of the tree now fading to gold. The decision she'd made in Georgia clung to her like southern heat—thick, inescapable, and full of consequence. She'd promised Grand Memaw. She'd looked into her eyes, seen the years and the pleading and the love, and said yes.

Yes, to Sunnyside.

Yes, to leaving Thunder Mountain.

Yes, to packing up everything she'd built and moving on.

And now the weight of that yes was settling deep in her bones.

Could she really walk away from this? From the work she loved, the people who trusted her, the town that had given her purpose? These folks had walked alongside her after her breakup with Merritt Hardwick—and as she recovered from alcohol addiction. They'd suffered with her through long childless years, after the quiet ache of watching other families grow while she stood still.

And then there were Charlie Grace, Lila, and Capri. The thought of miles separating them sent a shudder down her spine. These women had been her lifeline since high school. They rallied around her when she was the first black student to attend Thunder Mountain, paving the way for acceptance and friendship. They'd shared her life—the ups, the downs, and everything in between.

How could she possibly say goodbye?

She rubbed at her temples, trying to chase off the creeping ache.

Lucan's laughter broke into her thoughts, bright and

untamed. Her boy. Her miracle. She had to remember, this move wasn't just about honoring a promise—it was about giving him something too. Roots. Identity. A connection to a family heritage and a legacy shaped by soil and sweat and family.

Still, the cost was beginning to show.

A soft buzz from her phone pulled her from the fog. A message from her mother: *"Call when you can. We've started going through the back-office files and found something you'll want to see."*

Reva stared at the screen a moment longer, then set it aside. She wasn't ready for more news. Not yet.

Instead, she reached for the top folder on her desk, trying to lose herself in zoning requests and festival planning—anything to outrun the hollow ache of what was on the horizon.

12

Reva powered off the vacuum, the final hum dying into the warm hush of her mountain cabin. She stood for a moment, letting the stillness settle. Outside, the sun was dipping low behind the pines, casting gold across the windows and washing the reclaimed timber floors in a glow that made everything feel a little softer, a little more forgiving.

She had personally designed every inch of this house. Local river stone wrapped the fireplace, where a low fire flickered. Thick beams spanned the vaulted ceiling, their rugged elegance matched by the buttery leather sofas and wrought-iron fixtures she'd carefully chosen. It was mountain chic at its finest—refined, earthy, strong.

Reva paused, eyes drifting to the windows that framed her view of the Tetons. The peaks stood majestic, silhouetted against the last pink blush of twilight, and for a moment, it hit her all over again—what she was about to leave.

This house wasn't just beautiful. It was a sanctuary. Every stone and beam had been chosen with care, not just for style but for the life she had built inside its walls. She and Kellen had created a home here. Lucan had taken his first steps on this floor. Late nights of laughter and long talks with her girlfriends had echoed through this kitchen. This wasn't just a house—it was part of her story.

And soon...she would close this chapter.

She swallowed hard as she wound the cord around the vacuum and rolled it into the hall closet before heading toward the kitchen, the soles of her Golden Goose sneakers squeaking on polished wood. Her pace quickened a little. The girls would be arriving soon, and tonight had to be right.

The kitchen island gleamed, the slate and pearl swirls in the granite countertops a stark contrast against a bank of deep walnut cabinets. She opened the brown bag Kellen had dropped off an hour ago. Inside was the spread she'd ordered from Whistling Grizzly in Jackson, an array of hors d'oeuvres that made her stomach growl in anticipation.

Smoked steelhead dip with crisp crackers. Elk tartare, garnished with a quail egg and tiny capers. Bison bone marrow, roasted and glistening in its little ramekin boats. And her personal favorite—Cowboy Pops. Tender chunks of braised beef, marinated until spicy and sweet, grilled to perfection, then skewered and served on sticks.

She arranged everything on her largest charcuterie board, lit a few candles, and stepped back to assess.

Yes, she'd gone way beyond normal. But she wanted tonight to be special.

After all the emotional whiplash of the past few weeks, she needed this. A night to catch up with her girlfriends, to circle the wagons. To escape the outside world and be reminded they still had each other.

She reached for a bottle of sparkling water and popped the top. As the fizz settled, so did she, breathing in the scent of lemon and pine from the diffuser she'd tucked on the sideboard earlier. The front door would open soon. The laughter would start. And for a little while, the world might just feel normal again.

Reva set the last glass on the counter and stood back, smoothing a wrinkle from her blouse with a swipe of her palm. Everything was ready—candles flickering, playlist humming low in the background, and the spread from Whistling Grizzly arranged just so. She took one last look around, then paused as the soft glow of headlights swept across the living room walls.

There they were.

An engine cut off, followed by the sound of doors opening and the unmistakable cadence of familiar voices layered in laughter and overlapping chatter. Reva smiled to herself, her heart warming at the sound. No matter how much was shifting beneath her surface, this part—this right here—was solid.

She stepped toward the front door just as the doorbell rang, more out of habit than necessity.

When she opened it, the mountain air spilled in, crisp and scented with pine. Capri stood in front, bundled in a shearling coat with her long blonde hair tumbling around her face, talking over her shoulder to Lila, who was hauling a casserole dish and giving Charlie Grace a look that clearly meant *don't you dare drop that bottle of wine.*

"Evening, ladies," Reva said with a slow smile. "You're just in time. The elk tartare is chilling, and I'm two seconds from pouring the Prosecco."

"Girl," Charlie Grace grinned as she stepped inside, the warmth of the house rushing around them. "You always set the bar."

Lila handed off the dish—sweet potato puffs, by the smell of it—and leaned in to hug her. "It smells amazing in here."

Capri was last through the door, eyeing the interior with a casual glance that tried too hard to look unimpressed. "Okay, Mayor. Hosting game strong."

Reva laughed, motioning them in. "Come on. Coats in the

hallway, drinks in the kitchen, and I fully expect each of you to gush over my ridiculous overspending."

The kitchen filled quickly with the kind of ease that came only from years of friendship. Charlie Grace uncorked the wine, Lila grabbed plates, and Capri, despite claiming she wasn't hungry, immediately reached for a Cowboy Pop and moaned as she bit into it.

"I take it back," she said, chewing. "This was worth whatever you paid."

Reva smirked. "That's what I told Kellen. He didn't blink—just asked if there'd be leftovers."

Lila passed out the plates. "So, where is Kellen tonight?"

Reva placed a napkin holder on the counter next to the food. "He took Lucan to story time at Bluebird Books."

Lila nodded. "Ah, a favorite for all the little kiddos in Thunder Mountain." She reached for a cracker and dredged it generously through the bowl of smoked steelhead dip. "It's possible there won't be leftovers," she warned.

"I second that," Charlie Grace said, leaning one hip against the counter as she reached for the elk tartare. "I've never tasted anything so good."

Reva glanced over. "How's Jewel doing since the wildlife officials came and took the wolf pups?"

Charlie Grace's smile softened. "Better than I expected, honestly. The first few days were hard—lots of tears. She kept asking if they were scared without her, if they missed her singing at night."

Capri set down her glass. "Poor kid. That's tough."

"It was," Charlie Grace said. "But Fish and Game has been amazing. They let her visit the pups yesterday, and she got to help bottle-feed one of them. She's already talking about what she's going to wear when they let her be there for the release back into the wild."

Lila smiled. "That's special. What a memory she'll have."

"She calls it 'graduation day,'" Charlie Grace added with a laugh. "She's making each of her babies a 'certificate.' Hand-drawn and laminated."

"Oh, I love that," Reva said warmly. "She's such a bright light."

Charlie Grace nodded, her voice quieter. "She really is. And she's learning something important, too—about letting go, and still loving."

For a moment, they all sat with that—because they knew the lesson, too. Especially Reva.

Lila grinned, then grew thoughtful. "Speaking of babies...I want to throw Camille a shower."

Reva smiled at that. "That's a lovely idea."

"Nothing fancy," Lila said quickly. "Just something sweet before the baby comes. I thought we could do it at the community center, maybe serve brunch? Or should we wait until after she delivers?"

"I say before," Charlie Grace said. "Give her something to look forward to. You know we'll help."

"Definitely," Capri added, sipping from her glass. "And we'll make her laugh, which she needs."

"I know I was shocked when I first learned about the baby," Lila told them. "And goodness knows, it took a little effort for me to recalibrate what I imagined for my daughter's future. But now that I have...well, I'm looking forward to the arrival of her little one. And to being a grandma. The first amongst us, I might add." She grinned. "So let the party planning begin!"

The warmth around the island grew as the friends continued passing appetizers and tossing out ideas—decorations, games, whether Capri could be trusted not to spike the punch.

Then Lila's gaze settled on Reva. "How's your grandmother?" she asked gently. "Your earlier texts were encouraging. You said she was still hanging on."

Reva stiffened slightly, her fingers tightening around the stem of her glass. "She is. No real change. I'll probably head back again soon."

There was a quiet beat, an expectant silence hanging in the space between the words. The question behind the question lingered in Reva's mind, but she didn't answer it.

There would soon come a time...but not now. Not yet. For now, the decision would remain tucked between Kellen and her only.

Instead, she cleared her throat and reached for the serving spoon. "But I am worried about someone else right now."

All three women looked up.

"Fleet Southcott," Reva said. "I'm afraid he's been showing disturbing signs of memory loss. I planned to talk with him about it today, but he missed his afternoon meeting. His wife called him to remind him—it was on his calendar—but he still didn't show. This isn't the first time."

Charlie Grace frowned. "I heard from Nick that he came into the production office last week asking about permits he'd already signed months ago. Twice."

Capri leaned forward. "And he showed up to the school fundraiser wearing his pajama bottoms."

Lila's eyes widened. "Oh no."

"Oh yes," Reva said softly. "It's very troubling. His wife has made an appointment with a specialist in Cheyenne. But I think we all know something dreadful is going on with him."

The mood shifted, heavier now. Charlie Grace's voice dropped. "Do you think it's dementia?"

"I do," Reva said. "And it's getting worse. I'm already putting temporary precautions in place. Once confirmed, I'll have no choice but to replace him."

They were quiet a moment, all of them processing.

"But replacing Fleet?" Lila finally said. "That's a big deal. He's been sheriff since..."

"Twenty-two years," Capri said. "We were barely out of high school. And he swore Reva in as mayor, remember?"

"I remember," Reva said, her voice softer now. "Which is why this is gutting me."

Charlie Grace folded her arms. "If it were anyone else...but Fleet's the real deal. He loves this town."

"He *is* this town," Lila added.

"But what if someone gets hurt because he forgets something important?" Capri asked. "That's the part I can't shake."

They all nodded, each feeling the weight of it. The mix of loyalty and responsibility. Of heartbreak and leadership.

Reva drew in a breath. "It may come down to me having to make the call. But I need your support when I do. Not as mayor —but as your friend. As someone who's going to cry her eyes out the day I tell him."

Charlie Grace reached across the island, covering Reva's hand with hers. "You'll have it. All of it."

One by one, the others nodded, the silence now something sacred. A moment of truth among women who'd weathered many storms together—and were preparing, once again, to hold each other up.

13

Capri shut the door softly behind her, mindful of the late hour. The cozy scent of woodsmoke met her nose, followed by the rhythmic snip of scissors. Jake sat cross-legged in front of the fireplace, a small vise clamped to a low table, his hands now deftly wrapping copper wire and hackle around a tiny hook. The flickering flames cast golden light across the room, playing against the rugged slope of his cheek and the knit of concentration in his brow.

A slow smile crept across her face. She crossed the room and leaned down, pressing a gentle kiss to his cheek. "You do realize fly fishing season's just about over, right?"

Jake didn't look up right away. He tightened a loop, tested the line, then finally lifted his head, his eyes crinkling. "Nonsense," he said with the quiet authority she was starting to recognize as pure Jake. "In early fall, all the tributaries are open. Water levels might be lower, but that just means the fish are easier to find. Bigger ones are feeding up before winter, especially in those deeper pools where the current slows down. And hatches still happen when the sun warms things up in the afternoon. Trust me—if you go at the right time, the fish are biting."

Capri sank onto the floor beside him, watching as he reached for a tuft of elk hair and trimmed it expertly. The fire popped, and she pulled her knees up beneath her. "You always this convincing?" she asked, a half-teasing edge to her voice.

Jake glanced over, the corner of his mouth lifting. "Only when I know I'm right."

She leaned back, letting herself relax into the quiet hush of home, the hum of companionship, the soft crackle of the fire. For once, she didn't feel the need to fix or plan or prove anything. Jake had a way of grounding her like that—reminding her that the world could keep spinning without her at the helm.

"Teach me?" she asked after a pause.

He looked up, surprised, then nodded slowly. "I'd like that."

And though she didn't say it aloud, Capri thought she might like it, too.

Jake reached beside him and held out a second vise, sliding it across the table until it rested in front of her. "Here," he said, his voice low and steady. "This one's yours."

Capri hesitated, then scooted closer until their knees touched. She watched as he selected a hook and secured it in the clamp, then handed her a spool of thread. His fingers brushed hers—warm, calloused, sure—and a tingle zipped straight through her. She swallowed and steadied her breath.

"Start with a base layer," he murmured, guiding her hand in slow, precise movements. "You want to wrap the thread evenly, keep it tight, but not too tight. Like this."

He shifted behind her slightly, his arms coming around her sides, his hands over hers. His chin was near her shoulder, close enough that she could feel the warmth of his breath and the subtle scratch of his beard against her hairline. She followed his guidance, wrapping the thread slowly, her focus narrowing to the feel of his touch—firm but gentle, completely present.

It wasn't just about the fly. It was the way he taught her—patiently, quietly—as if there was nowhere else he'd rather be. And something about that undid her a little.

"You're good at this," she said softly, keeping her eyes on the vise to avoid the intensity of what she felt building inside.

"So are you," he replied. Then, after a pause, "Did you tell the girls we're going to set a date soon?"

The question floated into the warm hush of the room like a soft ripple on still water. She blinked, her hands stilling.

"No," she said, the answer honest and immediate. "I meant to. But between Reva's trip to Georgia, the baby shower plans, Fleet, and everything else...it felt like later might be better."

Jake didn't push. He just nodded, as if he understood more than she was saying.

"I didn't want to make it about me," Capri added, her voice quieter now. "Everyone's going through so much. I guess I thought...I'd wait until the moment felt right."

Jake leaned forward and kissed the spot just behind her ear. "When you're ready," he said simply.

And just like that, Capri felt a flicker of peace settle beneath her ribs—the kind that only came when someone knew how to hold both your hand and your heart without asking you to let go of either.

They sat together in silence for a moment, the fire painting shadows across the walls, the half-finished fly still caught in the vise between them.

Jake shifted slightly, his voice low. "I love you, you know."

Capri turned her head, studying him. His eyes held hers, steady and unflinching.

He set the thread spool down, then gently took her hands and pulled her to her feet. "Come here."

She stood, letting him draw her close. He kissed her, slow

and deep, his hands resting lightly on her hips. When he pulled back, she answered his non-verbal question with a smile.

Jake didn't need further encouragement. He took her hand, guiding her down the hallway.

"What about the flies?" she whispered.

His voice was a little rough. "They'll be there in the morning."

Inside the bedroom, he turned to face her, brushing his fingers through her long blonde hair, the strands slipping between his hands. His gaze searched hers, unspoken questions and promises hovering just beneath the surface.

Then her phone buzzed.

Capri's eyes fluttered closed, a groan rising in her throat. "Not now," she muttered, ignoring the intrusion.

Jake's hands moved gently down her arms, his touch grounding. But the phone buzzed again. And again.

She huffed, pulling away with visible frustration and grabbing the phone from her pocket. "What?"

Charlie Grace's voice came through the speaker, breathless and urgent. "Capri. Meet us at the hospital. It's Camille. Looks like she might be losing the baby."

Capri's heart thudded in her chest, her body already moving. She didn't need details—just the message. She met Jake's eyes, wide with worry.

"I have to go."

He was already pulling on his jacket. "I'm coming with you."

Together, they rushed from the house, the intimacy of moments before swept away by the force of something far more pressing—the fragile thread of new life, that of Lila's grandbaby, now hanging in the balance.

14

Lila sat motionless in the hard plastic chair outside the maternity ward, her hands clasped tightly in her lap. The antiseptic smell of the hospital made her stomach churn, but it was the silence that rattled her most—broken only by the distant beep of machines and the occasional overhead page.

She stared straight ahead, not seeing the scuffed tile or the faded brochure rack across from her. All she could see was Camille's face—pale, twisted with pain—as she'd helped her daughter into the car, trying not to panic at the blood, the way Camille had gasped and clutched her belly.

The doors at the end of the corridor banged open. Lila looked up as Charlie Grace, Reva, Jake, and Capri rushed in, hair windblown, faces flushed with urgency.

"Lila—" Charlie Grace dropped to her knees in front of her. "What happened?"

Lila's throat tightened. "I got home not long after we all left Reva's. Camille was doubled over in the bathroom. She said she felt cramping earlier but didn't want to worry me." She swallowed hard. "Then the bleeding started."

"Oh, Lila," Reva murmured, sliding into the chair beside her and wrapping an arm around her shoulders. "They are with her now?"

Lila nodded. "They rushed her into an exam room. Said a doctor would be in soon. I—I don't know anything yet."

Capri leaned against the wall, arms crossed tight over her chest, her voice soft but firm. "It could be a subchorionic hematoma. My cousin had one. Lots of bleeding. Sounds awful...but the baby was fine."

Jake moved to Capri's side, rubbed his stubbled chin. "I think we should think positive."

Charlie Grace nodded quickly, her thumbs racing over the tiny keyboard on her phone screen. "Says here it could be placenta previa—sometimes they just monitor it. Doesn't always mean the worst."

"She's seven months," Lila whispered. "Too early."

Reva gave her a gentle squeeze. "But far enough along that they'll do everything they can. Babies born this early can still thrive. You know that better than anyone."

Lila bit her lip, a tear sliding down her cheek. "I know. I do. But when it's your own child...and your grandchild—"

"We're here," Charlie Grace said, reaching for her hand. "You're not doing this alone."

The four women sat in a fragile circle of waiting—hearts racing, hope flickering, the bond between them stronger than ever in the face of the unknown.

Time passed in a haze of muted footsteps and the distant hum of machines. Lila couldn't say how long they sat there— ten minutes, maybe thirty—while the sterile walls closed in and her mind ran in frantic circles. She'd replayed it all again and again. Camille's moan of pain. The shaking hands that had packed her daughter's hospital bag just in case. The drive to Jackson, speeding through yellow lights with one hand on the wheel and the other reaching across the seat to touch Camille's knee, whispering, "Hold on, baby. Just hold on."

Charlie Grace pulled a bottle of water from her purse and pressed it into Lila's hands. Reva had taken over talking to the nurse at the front desk, checking for updates. Capri paced the length of the corridor more times than Lila could count, boots scuffing against the tile, while Jake sat with his elbows on his knees and stared at the floor.

Still no word. Still no doctor.

Then the double doors at the far end opened with a whoosh.

All four women stood at once. Jake too.

A man in blue scrubs stepped through, mask hanging loosely around his neck. He looked to be in his early forties, with dark eyes tired from too many late-night shifts. He paused when he saw them, then walked directly to Lila.

"Ms. Bellamy?" His voice was gentle.

Lila's mouth went dry. "Yes."

"I'm Dr. Reyes. I was the attending OB on call."

She nodded, legs suddenly weak.

He took a breath and pulled down the mask fully. "I'm so sorry. We did everything we could, but...the baby. The little girl didn't make it."

"A...a girl?" Lila's knees buckled, and Reva reached for her, guiding her back to the chair.

Dr. Reyes crouched slightly so they were eye-level. "Your daughter experienced a placental abruption. It happens when the placenta detaches from the uterine wall prematurely. It can lead to severe bleeding for both mother and baby. In Camille's case, it was rapid and complete."

Lila stared at him, the words slamming into her like a physical blow. "But she's—Camille?"

"She's stable," he said quickly. "We managed to stop the

bleeding. She's going to be okay. She doesn't know yet. We're waiting until she's more fully awake."

He hesitated. "We'll know more on the cause after some test results come back, but suffice it to say there was little we could do. I'm sorry."

Lila felt her body tremble. Her baby girl had lost her baby. A granddaughter she would never hold. A future that had just been ripped away before it even began.

Reva knelt in front of her, tears sliding silently down her cheeks. Charlie Grace and Capri stood close, hands on her shoulders.

There were no words. Only grief, raw and heavy, settling over them like a storm cloud with no break in sight.

15

The hallway outside Camille's room was quiet, hushed under the low hum of fluorescent lights. A nurse gave Lila a small nod as she passed, chart in hand. "She's awake."

Lila paused just outside the door, her hand resting on the handle. She wasn't sure she was ready. She wasn't sure Camille was ready. There was no blueprint for this kind of grief. Only love, and the aching pull to be near her daughter.

She eased the door open.

Camille was propped up against a stack of pillows, IV line in her arm, her skin pale against the hospital sheets. Her eyes—so much like her father's—met Lila's with a flicker of something unreadable. Not softness. Not quite anger. Something sharper. Wounded.

"Hey, sweetheart," Lila said gently as she stepped inside.

Camille turned her face toward the window. "They told me."

Lila's breath caught. "I'm so sorry."

A brittle laugh escaped Camille's throat. "Yeah, well. What's done is done."

"Camille—"

"There's nothing keeping me here now." Her voice was clipped, her gaze still fixed on the glass. "I'll call the university next week. Tell them I'm coming back. It's not too late to join the fall semester. I guess I should've never left."

Lila stepped closer to the bed. "Honey, it's okay to feel however you feel, but maybe give yourself a little time—"

"No." Camille turned then, her face stark with defiance. "You don't get it. I had plans. Big ones. This baby—" her voice caught, just for a second, then she swallowed it down, hard—"was never supposed to be part of the story. I let myself think I could do both. Be a mom and still chase a dream. But she must've known..."

Lila sat in the chair beside her and reached for her hand. "You're in shock. You're hurting. And it's okay to not know what to feel right now."

Camille yanked her hand away. "Don't."

Lila blinked, stung, but didn't move. "You've always had fire, Camille. You came into this world strong-willed and fearless. And you faced the unthinkable with your dad. All while remaining sweet...remaining you. I love that about you. But you don't have to be strong right now. You don't have to know what's next today."

Camille looked down at her lap, the bravado wavering.

"I know what it's like to lose something you didn't expect to forfeit," Lila said, her voice barely above a whisper. "You think charging ahead will dull the ache. But it won't."

A long silence passed between them.

Finally, Camille spoke. "I feel empty."

Lila reached out again, slower this time, her palm open on the edge of the bed.

Camille stared at it, then tentatively laid her hand in her mother's.

"I'm here," Lila said. "And I'll be here—through all of it.

Whether you stay, go back to school, chase dreams, or fall apart first. I'm not going anywhere."

And this time, her daughter didn't pull away.

Camille was discharged from the hospital two days later. Lila brought her home, set her up in the guest room with soft blankets and ginger tea, and waited—for a shift, for a crack in the armor, for her daughter to crumble in a way that invited comfort.

But it didn't come.

Instead, Camille moved through the house like a ghost, quiet and determined. She answered calls from her professors, sent emails confirming her return to campus, and by the fifth morning, she had her bags packed and stacked by the door.

There'd been no real conversation, no closure—just the hollow logistics of moving forward.

And so, less than a week after losing the baby, Camille climbed into her compact car and pulled out of the driveway with her eyes on the horizon and her heart locked up tight. Lila stood on the porch, arms wrapped around herself, watching the taillights until they disappeared down the winding road. She'd waved, forced a smile. Even managed a cheery, "Text when you stop for gas," though her voice had cracked at the end.

After the car was gone, the silence came rushing in.

Lila made her way down the gravel path to the mailbox, craving something—anything—to fill the emptiness. Perhaps she should try and meet up with one of the girls for lunch.

Inside, tucked between a real estate flyer and an electric bill, was a single ivory envelope. Heavy stock. A formal monogram engraved on the flap in raised gold lettering.

She opened it slowly, her fingers trembling. The card inside was crisp, impersonal.

"I'm sorry to learn of your loss. Sincerely, Senator Claudia Newcomb."

No return address. No warmth. No mention of Camille's name.

Lila stood there for a long moment, the breeze stirring her hair as she stared down at the card. Somehow, the cool politeness of it hit harder than she'd expected.

She folded it once, then again, and slipped it back into the envelope. Her eyes burned, but no tears came.

Instead, she turned and walked slowly back to the house—each step measured, her arms hanging limp at her sides. Her daughter was gone. Her granddaughter never had a chance. And the woman who chose to never be part of their future had sent regrets written in gold.

16

Reva steered her shiny black Escalade up the narrow pine tree-lined lane, the tires crunching over a thick layer of fallen needles and leaves. Sunlight filtered through the branches in golden threads, dappling the windshield and catching in her braided hair like a halo. The road curved gently, then widened into a clearing, revealing the house she'd visited more times over the years than she could count.

Modest, sturdy, and well-loved, the home stood with quiet dignity—a wood-framed structure stained a deep brown, its green shutters slightly faded from seasons of sun and snow. A small, covered porch jutted from the front, its floorboards weathered and a little crooked. A pair of rocking chairs flanked the door, their paint peeling at the arms where hands had rested for years.

Behind the house, the tin roof of a stock shed glinted in the light. Beyond it, a wire fence contained a handful of sheep, lazily grazing at the feeding trough. One lifted its head at the sound of her engine, then returned to chewing.

Reva parked and turned off the engine.

She didn't move right away. Just sat there with the engine off, the ticking of the cooling motor the only sound in the quiet clearing. Her gaze drifted to the front yard, scattered with crisp fall leaves. A child's swing set sat off to one side, its frame slightly rusted but still upright, two plastic swings twisting idly in the wind.

Reva exhaled slowly and leaned her head back against the seat. She hadn't wanted to come here. Not today. Not this way.

And still, she'd come. Because duty had a voice louder than her emotions.

Reva rubbed her palms down her thighs, smoothing imaginary wrinkles from her slacks. She straightened, eyes narrowing slightly as her hand reached for the door handle.

Reva climbed out of the car and closed the door behind her.

June Southcott stepped out onto the porch, letting the door ease shut behind her. She wasn't what folks might call flashy—never had been—but there was a simple grace about her that spoke of strong roots and deep love. Her gray-blonde hair was pulled back into a low twist, a few wisps lifting in the breeze. She wore a soft denim button-down over a long-sleeved cotton tee, the collar gently frayed from washings. Her jeans were clean but well-worn, and her brown leather shoes looked like they'd seen more than a few gardens and grocery aisles.

A faded dish towel was still tucked into her waistband, and Reva had a sudden, vivid memory of being a teenager and sitting at this very table inside, hands curled around a mug of tea, June fussing quietly in the kitchen with that same towel slung over her shoulder. She hadn't changed much. A little older maybe. A little thinner around the face. But the kindness was still there.

June stepped down from the porch, her eyes meeting Reva's as she crossed the lawn with steady steps. Leaves swirled around her ankles as she walked.

"Hey there, Reva," June said softly.

Her voice was warm, like a hand on the back of Reva's heart. But there was something behind it, too—something quieter. A kind of bracing. As if they both knew this day had a shape to it neither wanted to outline.

Reva's throat thickened, but she managed a small nod.

June didn't waste time with pretense. She reached for Reva's hand and held it. "Fleet's out back."

The older woman led Reva inside and to a kitchen table where she offered her a seat and a cup of coffee.

The kitchen smelled faintly of cinnamon and apples. June moved with practiced ease, retrieving two mugs from the open shelf above the sink and pouring coffee from a thermal carafe. The mugs didn't match—one was plain white, the other had a faded rooster on the side—but they felt right somehow.

Reva wrapped her hands around the warm ceramic, grateful for something to hold. She took a sip, letting the heat anchor her as June sat across from her.

Then came the sound of boots on the back steps. Slow. Measured.

The screen door creaked open, and a moment later, Fleet Southcott appeared in the doorway, backlit by the morning light. "Reva, what are you doing here?" He glanced at his wife. "Did I know she was coming?"

June shook her head.

Reva stood slowly, unsure if she should smile or brace herself. "Hi, Fleet."

For a beat, neither moved. Then his expression softened, lines easing at the corners of his eyes. "You didn't have to come all the way out here."

"I did," she said quietly.

And in that moment, they both knew this wasn't just a visit. It was something more.

∽

Reva pushed open the door to her office and stepped inside. She didn't bother flipping on the lights. The morning sun slanted through the tall windows, casting stripes across the carpeted floor and highlighting the fine dust on her desk that always settled no matter how often Verna insisted on wiping down the surface.

She let her purse slide off her shoulder into the side chair near the window and stood there a beat longer than she meant to, one hand resting against her chest. Finally, she turned and crossed to the credenza, eyes locked on the familiar silver carafe.

The first cup she'd had at the Southcotts' hadn't been enough. Not by half.

She poured herself a second and didn't bother with cream this time. Just the dark, bitter brew. She took a sip, felt it settle, and closed her eyes.

The soft patter of footsteps preceded the inevitable.

Verna Billingsley appeared in the doorway, holding a file folder and wearing the same burgundy pantsuit she'd worn to the town council meeting two nights ago. Her expression was tight with curiosity, though she did her best to soften it with a half-smile.

"How'd it go?"

Reva swallowed. She took another sip and then nodded, more to herself than anyone else.

"He took it graciously," she said, her voice low. "Like maybe he sensed it was coming. Maybe he's known for a while." She moved to her desk and sank into the chair, cradling the mug between her palms. "I explained the town council voted unanimously. He'll receive full retirement benefits, and I made sure he knows he'll always carry the title of *Honorary Sheriff* for life."

Verna stepped inside, the file forgotten in her arms. "And?"

"I told him Thunder Mountain would never forget what he's given us. That for more than two decades, he's been the backbone of this place—showing up in snowstorms, answering calls in the middle of the night, standing watch at every parade, every holiday gathering, every tragedy. I reminded him that kids feel safe because they know Fleet Southcott is out there. That families sleep easier because of him."

Her voice broke slightly, but she pushed through.

"He just nodded and said, 'I reckon a man can't catch all the bad guys when he can't remember where he put his keys.'"

Verna smiled sadly. "That sounds like Fleet."

Reva nodded. "Then June squeezed his hand and said, 'Keys can be found. Kindness can't easily be taught.'"

They stood in silence for a moment, the heaviness settling like a blanket.

Verna finally cleared her throat and stepped forward, placing the folder on Reva's desk. "You did the right thing. For him. For the town."

"I know," Reva murmured.

But knowing didn't make it easier.

17

The sharp jingle of the bell above the door rang out as Charlie Grace stepped into Wylie's Feed and Seed, brushing dust from her jeans. The familiar tang of hay, rubber boots, and motor oil clung to the air inside the store —just the kind of place she'd grown up feeling at home. She gave a quick wave to the calico cat perched on a stack of mineral lick tubs near the register.

Wylie Martin stood behind the counter, rearranging seed packets with the slow precision of a man who'd owned the store since before Charlie Grace could ride a two-wheeler. "Morning, Charlie Grace. Let me guess—something broke, and you're fixing it yourself instead of calling one of those ranch hands you keep on payroll."

She grinned and hefted a heavy-duty posthole digger onto the counter. "The south fence line near the creek got flattened in the windstorm last week. Figured I'd replace a few posts and re-tension the wire before the horses figure out there's an escape route."

Wylie raised one white brow and gave the digger a skeptical once-over. "You know, most folks in your position don't spend their morning digging in the mud. They write a check and call it good. Especially ones with bank accounts so full they burst."

"I know." Charlie Grace shrugged, brushing a strand of windblown hair from her face. "Old habits. Besides, it clears my head."

"Mmm." Wylie rang up the sale and slid the receipt across the counter. "Just don't forget—there's a difference between being capable and being stubborn. One makes you strong. The other just makes you tired."

She chuckled, pocketing her change. "Story of my life."

He leaned his elbows on the counter. "You ever think maybe it's time to let someone else shoulder a little of it? Lot of good men and women around here who'd jump at the chance."

Charlie Grace paused, her fingers tightening on the wooden handle of the posthole digger. "Maybe," she said, but her voice carried the weight of a woman not quite ready to admit it.

As she turned to leave, Wylie called out, "You'll have to learn sometime, Charlie Grace. Even the strongest horses need rest."

She gave him a two-finger salute and pushed through the door, the bell jingling again behind her.

Outside, the wind had picked up, carrying with it the smell of damp earth and wild sage. Charlie Grace loaded the tool into the bed of her truck.

She had just tugged the tailgate shut when a familiar wedge of sleek black metal nosed into a parking space across the street. She straightened, squinting into the sunlight as Nick Thatcher stepped out of his SUV, tall and trim in a flannel shirt rolled to the elbows and worn jeans that still somehow looked designer. A camera hung from his neck, the strap worn from use, his dark hair tousled by the wind.

He spotted her and grinned—wide, easy, and just a little crooked—then jogged across Main Street, dodging a passing pickup and drawing more than one glance from the Knit Wit ladies congregated on the bench outside the bakery.

"Thought that was your truck," he said as he approached, giving the posthole digger in the bed a curious glance. "You starting a landscaping business on the side?"

Charlie Grace leaned against the tailgate, a half-smile tugging at her lips. "Just doing repairs after the storm. South fence line took a hit."

Nick rested a hand on the edge of the truck, close but not touching her. "Of course, you are."

For the benefit of anyone watching—and more than a few were—he didn't lean in for a kiss, but the warmth in his eyes made it clear he could've. Charlie Grace felt it, the way she always did.

They'd met the year before when Nick stayed at her guest ranch while scouting locations for *Bear Country*, a gritty wilderness television show that had since become a breakout hit. As the show's production designer, Nick had every reason to move on after filming wrapped near Jackson—but he hadn't. He kept showing up. Kept calling. And somewhere along the line, their story had gone from casual to something neither of them could quite define, but both were reluctant to let go.

"You here scouting?" she asked, nodding toward the camera.

"Sort of," he said. "Thought I'd grab some shots of Thunder Mountain for an upcoming promotion campaign. You know I've got a soft spot for this place."

She rolled her eyes, but her voice softened. "Still trying to sneak it into season two?"

"I'm a patient man," he said, lifting the camera and snapping a photo before she could protest.

Charlie Grace gave him a look. "Delete it."

"Not a chance," he said. "You look like the kind of woman

who knows how to handle a fence post and then take on the world."

She shook her head, but she was smiling now. And for just a moment, she forgot all about broken fences and stubborn pride.

Nick tilted his head toward the corner. "Come on. Let me buy you a cup of coffee. Just ten minutes."

Charlie Grace hesitated, glancing toward the bed of her truck like the posthole digger might get up and do the work without her. "I've got a list a mile long, Nick. Fence repairs, and guests arriving this afternoon..."

"All still waiting when you're done," he said, sliding his sunglasses up onto his head. "There's no reason not to say yes."

The corners of her mouth tugged, despite her best effort to keep them neutral. "You always this pushy?"

"When I know what I want."

He extended a hand—open, easy—and waited.

Charlie Grace eyed it for a beat. Then she exhaled and placed her palm in his.

His fingers wrapped around hers like a promise—warm, steady, and sure. The kind of touch that didn't ask for anything, just offered presence. The wood-planked sidewalk creaked beneath their boots as they made their way toward the Rustic Pine, the storefronts lined with potted mums.

She tried not to notice how perfectly their strides matched, how natural it felt to walk hand in hand like they'd been doing it for years. But she did notice. The rough callus at the base of his thumb, the way his hand tightened ever so slightly when they passed Nicola Cavendish and her yap-happy Yorkie.

She should've felt guilty for taking the detour. Should've felt antsy, already planning how to make up for lost time. Instead, her heart felt a little lighter, like maybe the world could wait ten more minutes.

Maybe even longer.

The Rustic Pine was only half full, the quiet hum of locals nursing second cups of coffee and chatting over breakfast.

Charlie Grace followed Nick inside and immediately spotted Pete Cumberland behind the bar, refilling a saltshaker. Annie, bustling near the kitchen pass-through with her signature half-apron and easy smile, waved them over.

"Morning, you two," Pete called out. "Didn't expect to see you out and about this early, Charlie Grace. Heard you were neck-deep in postholes and barbed wire."

"I was," she said with a chuckle, then nodded toward Nick. "But someone had other ideas."

Pete arched a brow at Nick, grinning. "Good man."

"Hey, I caught your sermon on Sunday," Nick added. "The bit about sowing in hard soil? That landed."

Pete gave a modest shrug. "Well, I reckon if it stuck with you, then the good Lord must've had His hand in it. I just try to stay out of the way and say what needs saying."

Annie stepped in, wiping her hands on a towel. "Sit wherever you'd like. I'll bring two cups of the good stuff." She winked at Charlie Grace. "We made that Guatemalan roast you like."

They slid into a corner booth near the window, sunlight slanting across the table in soft golden beams. True to her word, Annie returned moments later with two steaming mugs, the aroma rich and nutty.

Charlie Grace cupped hers between her hands, savoring the warmth. "I forgot how good this feels—just sitting."

Nick blew across the surface of his coffee, then leaned back and gave her that look. The one that saw too much. "Maybe you should do it more often."

Before she could reply, her phone buzzed against the table. She glanced at the screen—a quick text from Jewel's riding instructor, confirming a lesson reschedule.

She typed a reply, set the phone down, and barely exhaled before it buzzed again.

Another message. This time from one of her ranch hands asking about a delivery.

Charlie Grace reached for it, already rehearsing instructions in her head, but Nick gently caught her hand and instead slid the phone across the table, out of reach.

"Just a few minutes," he said softly. "That's all I'm asking. Be here. With me."

She blinked at him, caught off guard by the kindness in the gesture more than the act itself. Her fingers, still half-stretched toward the phone, curled back into her palm.

"I'm not great at putting things down," she admitted, her voice low.

Nick took a sip of coffee, eyes on hers. "Then start with this."

They sat in companionable silence for a moment, the clink of forks and the low murmur of conversation filling the Rustic Pine around them. Charlie Grace wrapped both hands around her mug, stared into it for a beat, then looked up at Nick, eyes clear and direct.

"All right," she said, her voice low but steady. "You asked for ten minutes, so here it is. No holding back."

She took a breath and launched in, her words tumbling out faster than she expected. "The other day, Reva, Capri, and I met at Lila's to take down the nursery…"

Nick's expression filled with tenderness. "I'm listening."

"Camille's gone back to school, and…well." She didn't finish the sentence. She didn't have to. She looked across the table and shook her head. "All our hearts are breaking for Lila— grieving a loss no woman should ever have to endure. And yet, she moves through each day with a quiet strength that doesn't come from willpower or bravery, but from the simple, brutal fact that she doesn't have a choice. Life keeps going, whether you're ready or not. And Lila, somehow, keeps going too."

Nick was quiet for a moment, his fingers tracing the rim of his coffee mug. Then he looked at her, his expression softer than she'd ever seen it. "You're a good friend, Charlie Grace. Don't underestimate how much that matters, even when you and the others can't fix it."

"Reva took everything—crib, rocking chair, even the little bins with woodland animals on the front. Said she'd make sure it all went to good homes. You should've seen the way she loaded it all into her SUV like she was prepping for a covert mission."

Nick chuckled, but Charlie Grace shook her head, eyes soft. "Something's off with Reva, though. She had to let Fleet Southcott go. Nearly broke her heart. And I think the thing with her Grand Memaw is hitting her harder than she's letting on. Reva always carries more than she shows."

She paused, then leaned back in the booth. "You know, back in high school, she once organized a fundraiser car wash for the debate team because the school cut their budget. She made all of us wear swimsuits and tank tops—said the boys would drive through twice if we did."

Nick laughed. "Did it work?"

"Oh, it worked. Raised over eight hundred dollars in one Saturday. But here's the best part—Reva convinced our principal it was educational. Said it was 'applied persuasive strategy in a real-world economic context.'" Charlie Grace grinned at the memory. "The woman's been talking her way into impossible solutions since we were sixteen."

She sobered then, her voice quieting. "But lately, it's like her spark is dimmed. I just...I don't know. I hate not knowing how to help."

Nick reached across the table, his fingers brushing hers.

"Maybe just being there is enough right now. Sometimes that's all people need."

Charlie Grace nodded, grateful. But in her chest, something stirred—like a thread pulling tight between her desire to be there for her friends and the helplessness of not knowing how. She hated that feeling—of standing on the sidelines when all she wanted was to fix something, anything.

Nick seemed to sense the tug-of-war inside her. His gaze softened, then brightened with a flicker of something playful.

"I've got just the thing you need right now," he said.

Charlie Grace arched a brow. "What?"

He leaned back, lips tugging into a grin. "It's a surprise. But be ready Saturday morning. I'm picking you up. No ifs, ands, or buts. It's a date."

She gave a mock sigh. "Fine. But what am I wearing to this mysterious cure-all?"

Nick's eyes drifted over her, slow and deliberate, a smile playing at the corners of his mouth. "Just what you've got on is fine."

She narrowed her eyes, amused. "So...mud-splattered and mildly exhausted?"

He laughed. "Exactly. Wouldn't want you any other way."

18

Capri stirred beneath the quilt, the morning sun slipping through the cracks in the blinds and warming her bare shoulder. She reached for Jake, but her hand met only cool sheets. A sigh whispered from her lips—half disappointment, half curiosity. She sat up, brushing her hair out of her face.

And then she saw it.

A tray rested on the bedside table, carefully balanced and waiting. Two cinnamon rolls glistened under a soft drizzle of icing, and next to them sat a tall glass of orange juice, already beading with condensation. A small white vase held a single sunflower—bright, cheerful, and unapologetically bold.

Just like Jake.

Her breath caught, then released in a soft, surprised laugh. She traced the rim of the glass with one finger, her gaze landing on the sunflower. She didn't need grand gestures. This was enough. This was everything.

Her phone rested on the nightstand; screen dark until she picked it up. An idea bloomed—quick and unpolished, the way most good ones were. With her thumb, she tapped out a short message.

"Hey. I just had a crazy idea. Want to get married this weekend?"

She stared at the message for half a beat longer, then tapped *Send* before she could overthink it.

Then she waited.

THE EARLY MORNING sun spilled across the paddock as Charlie Grace leaned on the fence rail and watched Jewel climb on the school bus at the end of the lane. In the corral, the horses moved lazily, tails swishing at flies, and somewhere behind her, Clancy's radio played an old country tune through the open window. She gave a wave to Donna Hatfield, the bus drive before climbing down and heading for the house. On the way, her phone buzzed in her jeans back pocket. She pulled it out, shielding the screen from the glare.

"It's my turn to host this Friday night. Be at my house. Six o'clock sharp."

A smile curved her lips. Capri was back, all business and no room for excuses.

At the same time, Lila stood at the counter at the clinic, sipping coffee from her travel mug while reviewing the day's appointments.

The clinic was quiet in that rare, golden window before the day began—no ringing phones, no barking dogs, just the hum of the mini fridge and the distant sound of Whit moving around in the back.

Her phone lit up beside the keyboard. She tapped the screen and read the message. *"It's my turn to host this Friday night. Be at my house. Six o'clock sharp."*

She smiled, setting down the mug. There was nothing she loved more than time with her girlfriends.

Reva stood in front of the community center bulletin board, a fresh stack of flyers in one hand and a roll of painter's tape in the other. Lucan darted across the hallway, making truck noises with a paper cup.

Her phone buzzed inside her blazer pocket. She fished it out and scanned the incoming text.

"It's my turn to host this Friday night. Be at my house. Six o'clock sharp."

Reva arched a brow, a grin tugging at the corners of her mouth. "Well, well," she murmured to herself, clicking off the phone. "Capri playing hostess and barking orders? Business as usual."

TIRES CRUNCHED along the gravel as the three vehicles paraded down Capri's lane and pulled into her yard. One by one, Lila, Charlie Grace, and Reva stepped out, the crisp mountain air tugging at their jackets as they headed for the porch.

Charlie Grace adjusted the hem of her flannel shirt. "What are the odds there's anything edible involved?"

Lila laughed. "If Capri ordered takeout, I'll count it as progress."

"I brought wine," Reva added, holding up a bag. "Because even if she *did* cook, we might need it."

The front door creaked open, and to their surprise, Annie Cumberland stepped onto the porch, her cheeks pink with excitement. "Ladies," she called with a twinkle in her eye, "this way, please. To the backyard."

The trio exchanged puzzled glances, but there was no time to ask questions. Annie was already disappearing around the corner of the house, motioning for them to keep up.

They trailed after her, steps quickening with each stride. But nothing—not the casual text, not the breezy invitation—

could've prepared them for what they saw when they turned the corner.

They stopped cold.

Charlie Grace actually gasped. "What in the..."

Lila blinked as if she'd walked into the wrong yard. "Is that—?"

"Oh, my Lord," Reva breathed. "She's getting *married*."

A simple arch made of twisted willow branches stood near the edge of the garden, its natural curve softened with sprays of golden mums, ivory ranunculus, rust-colored zinnias, and deep burgundy dahlias. Clusters of baby's breath and seeded eucalyptus were tucked between the blooms, giving it an unstudied elegance—like something you might stumble upon in a fairy tale.

Charlie Grace blinked hard. "No way."

Lila covered her mouth. "Oh my gosh..."

Reva whispered, "I never suspected this."

At the base of the arch, Jake stood with his hands folded in front of him. He wore jeans and cowboy boots, a clean button-up under a simple jacket. No tie. No fuss. Just calm, quiet confidence—and eyes searching the path for only one person.

They exchanged quick greetings and moved into the space where Annie directed before she stepped to one side, lifted her violin, and began to play the first delicate notes of *Canon in D Major*. The melody floated through the trees like spun gold.

Then Capri appeared.

She stepped barefoot into the clearing, her white eyelet Gunne Sax dress fluttering around her ankles. The delicate sleeves clung to her arms, and the skirt swayed with each quiet step. Her blonde hair loosely cascaded around her shoulders, adorned with tiny white asters and sprigs of lavender, as if she'd gathered wildflowers from the fields that morning and had woven them in.

She looked radiant. Untamed. Exactly like herself.

Jake's breath visibly caught as she came toward him, her eyes locked on his. The girlfriends stood side by side, too moved to speak. Reva reached out and hooked pinkies with Lila. Charlie Grace swiped at her cheek and muttered something about how beautiful Capri looked.

Pastor Pete cleared his throat, then smiled at the tiny gathering. "We weren't given much notice," he said warmly, "but when love taps you on the shoulder and says *now*, it's best not to keep it waiting."

Capri gave a soft laugh that trembled at the edges.

Jake reached for her hands, cradling them in his own.

Pete's words fell gently into the hush—about trust and timing, and the beauty of choosing one another, not just once, but again and again. Capri's eyes shimmered, and when Jake repeated his vows, slow and sure, her chin trembled.

When it was her turn, she didn't read from a paper. She just looked up at him and whispered, "You're the calm in my storm. And the one place I never expected to feel safe. But I do."

Tears tracked silently down Lila's face. Reva blinked fast, failing miserably at holding it together. Charlie Grace didn't even try.

Pete smiled. "By the power vested in me, and witnessed by the people who matter most, I now pronounce you husband and wife. Jake—you may kiss your bride."

Jake pulled Capri into his arms and kissed her like a man who never intended to let go.

And just like that, under a willow arch and the blush of fall flowers, Capri Jacobs—wild, bossy, broken, and brave—became a wife.

19

Word of Capri's surprise wedding spread through Thunder Mountain faster than spring melt on the Snake River. By Monday morning, it was all anyone could talk about—at the post office, the feed store, even during Pastor Pete's sermon, where he'd barely made it to the benediction without veering into a reflection on love and willow arches.

Everyone had an opinion—from Nicola Cavendish, who claimed she "just knew something was brewing," to Albie Barton, who declared it the most romantic thing since the barn dance of '97. Capri, of course, refused to indulge the fuss, but the glint in her eye said she didn't mind one bit.

Despite her usual resistance to being the center of attention, Capri finally caved under the relentless pressure from her girlfriends—and maybe a little coaxing from Jake. She agreed to a celebration at the Rustic Pine, insisting on "simple and low-key," which everyone promptly ignored.

Annie Cumberland cleared the back room, stringing white lights across the beams and hauling out mason jars filled with wildflowers. The Knit Wit ladies volunteered to bake pies,

Pastor Pete promised a toast that wouldn't make her squirm, and even Clancy Rivers offered to play a song or two on his harmonica—though no one could remember the last time he'd played in key.

The moment Jake pushed open the door to the Rustic Pine, warm light and laughter spilled onto the front porch like a welcome mat. Capri stepped inside beside him, and the room erupted.

"Woooooo! That's our girl!" hollered Pastor Pete from behind the bar. He wore his signature denim apron over a button-up shirt and raised a glass as the applause swelled.

Annie, cheeks flushed and curls bouncing, stood on top of a wooden crate near the jukebox and let out a piercing whistle. "All right, settle down now! Newlyweds comin' through!"

The crowd parted like the Red Sea, revealing faces Capri had known her whole life.

Charlie Grace was waving a cloth napkin in the air like she was at a rodeo. "Well look at you, Mrs. Carrington!" she called with a grin.

Capri blushed as Jake took her hand and led her in. "I don't think I've ever been applauded for entering a bar before," she murmured.

"Guess there's a first time for everything," Jake said, giving her hand a squeeze.

Oma stood near the back, holding a platter of deviled eggs with one hand and dabbing her eyes with a tissue in the other. "I knew it," she whispered to no one in particular. "I just knew love would find her."

Lila elbowed her way to the front with a tray of lemon bars. "You look radiant," she said, handing one to Capri before taking a bite of her own. "And I don't use that word lightly."

"I think it's the barefoot bride thing," Reva chimed in, appearing beside her in a flowy purple dress, holding her son Lucan on her hip. "Totally your brand."

"Y'all, give them room!" Annie said again, leaping down from her crate and ushering Capri and Jake toward the center of the room. "We've got a night to remember planned."

The Rustic Pine had never looked more festive. Twinkly lights crisscrossed the ceiling, looped with garlands of cotton bolls, pine cones, and autumn leaves. Mismatched chairs circled every table, each one topped with platters of food brought by nearly every family in town.

Nicola Cavendish, in a floor-length red wrap dress that shimmered like sequins under the lights, floated over with Sweetpea tucked under one arm. "I told Wooster this morning we were due for a town wedding. I *knew* this was coming. Oh, and look at your hair, Capri—it's practically Grecian."

"Thank you, Nicola," Capri said, catching Reva's smirk.

Jake was soon pulled into a circle of men near the bar—Fleet Southcott, Clancy Rivers, Albie Barton, and Nick Thatcher among them—who were already debating which of them cried harder at the ceremony—Reva, Lila, or Charlie Grace.

"I got dust in my eye," Charlie Grace said as she joined them. She pointed a finger at Jake. "But you—*you* looked downright choked up."

Jake laughed and shook his head. "Guilty."

Capri turned, only to be scooped into a hug by Jewel, Charlie Grace's daughter, who handed her a crumpled watercolor painting. "I made this for you," she said proudly. "It's you and Jake and six dogs and a unicorn."

Capri blinked. "That is...very accurate."

"And there's a fish wearing a veil," Jewel added, pointing.

"Even better."

Annie made her way to the front of the room with her violin in hand. She tapped her bow against her palm, and the room quieted.

"Capri and Jake," she said, her voice warm. "We watched

you two fall for each other—some of us slower than others," she added with a wink at Capri, who rolled her eyes as laughter rippled through the crowd. "But all of us have enjoyed watching this love story unfold. So, from our hearts to yours, this night is for you."

She lifted the violin to her chin and began to play. The opening strains of "What a Wonderful World" drifted through the room, quieting the conversations. Couples reached for one another. Charlie Grace leaned her head on Nick's shoulder. Lila dabbed her eyes.

When the song ended, Annie stepped back, gave a theatrical bow, and then grinned.

"Now for a little fun," she declared. With a flick of her wrist, she transitioned from violin to fiddle, and a rollicking mountain tune kicked up. The change in the room was instant.

Lucan squealed and clapped.

"Yeehaw!" yelled Bodhi West, already hauling his girlfriend toward the makeshift dance floor, which had been cleared in front of the fireplace.

The Knit Wit ladies shuffled out in matching shawls, forming a line.

"Capri, come on!" Charlie Grace said, grabbing her hand.

"I don't know the steps," Capri protested.

"Doesn't matter. Just stomp and laugh."

And she did. They all did.

The night unfolded like a living postcard of everything Capri never knew she'd wanted. Jake twirled her once, then again. Her hair fell from its twist. She didn't care.

Later, she stood with a cider in hand, breathless from dancing, while Pete clinked a spoon against a glass to get everyone's attention.

"I've got just one more thing to say," he said. "In a town like this, we celebrate our own. We don't always do it perfectly. But we show up. And tonight, we showed up for a girl who once said she'd never get married, and a guy who came to town with a hammer and a good heart."

He looked over at Capri. "We love you, sweetheart. And we love that you let us be part of this."

Capri felt Jake's hand slip around her waist. She rested her head against his shoulder, overcome.

It didn't matter that her mother or Dick weren't there to raise a glass—God had given her an extended family in these people, and as she looked around the Rustic Pine, her heart was full to the brim.

As the night wore on, plates were scraped clean, cake was served (homemade by Annie, who wouldn't reveal her frosting secret), and laughter floated out onto the darkened street.

Reva and Kellen slow danced near the jukebox. Lila dozed with her head on Whit's shoulder. Clancy held Sweetpea in one hand and a root beer float in the other, looking entirely content.

Capri stepped outside for a breath of air and found herself staring up at a sky pricked with stars. Jake followed and wrapped his arms around her.

"You okay?" he asked softly.

She nodded, her voice catching. "Yeah. Just...I didn't think I'd ever have this."

Jake pressed a kiss to her temple. "It was always waiting. You just had to stop running."

Behind them, the fiddle music rose again, and someone—probably Pastor Pete—let out a whoop loud enough to wake the dead.

Capri smiled. "Come on," she said, taking Jake's hand. "Let's go back in. This is our town. And tonight, Thunder Mountain is throwing one heck of a party."

20

Charlie Grace checked her reflection in the side mirror of her truck, ran a hand through her curls, then laughed at herself. "It's not that big of a deal—only a date," she murmured, though her heart clearly hadn't gotten the memo.

While their original plan got delayed by a surprise wedding, Nick had adjusted with ease andrescheduled. "Dress comfortable," he'd added with that maddening half-grin that always made her suspicious. And intrigued.

She pulled into the gravel driveway leading to Nick's place —a log-sided home tucked near the tree line on the west side of Jackson, where the valley floor met the rise of lodgepole and fir. The house looked like something out of a Robert Redford film —sturdy and handsome, with a front porch strung in market lights and a stack of firewood piled with precision.

Before she could knock, the front door opened and Nick stepped out, coffee in one hand, a red-checkered bandana in the other. He wore dark jeans and a lightweight, zip-up canvas jacket over a white T-shirt, the kind that looked like it had seen a few adventures. His boots were broken-in leather, clean but clearly lived-in. The morning breeze ruffled his hair, and the glint of aviator sunglasses tucked into his jacket pocket was the only nod to anything out of the ordinary—except for the goofy expression that said he was far too pleased with himself.

"Well," he said, handing her the bandana, "you're right on time."

She raised a brow. "On time for what?"

Nick grinned. "We've got an adventure to chase."

Her pulse skipped. "Are you finally going to show me how to use your Leica M3?"

"Tempting," he said. "But no—no cameras today. We're heading somewhere. Come on."

They climbed into his truck, and Nick wouldn't say a word about their destination. Just fiddled with the radio, humming along to old country tunes and occasionally glancing her way like a man carrying a secret in his chest.

After thirty minutes and a winding drive up a forest road, they came to a spot where Nick shut off the engine, climbed out, and came around to open her door.

"Ready?"

She gave him a slow smile. "I'm not sure."

The sound of gravel crunching under her boots echoed in the silence as she followed Nick down a narrow path through the trees. They emerged into a sun-drenched clearing—and there it was. A small silver aircraft sat on a makeshift airstrip of mown grass, its polished nose gleaming in the morning light like something out of an old postcard.

Charlie Grace stopped in her tracks. "Nick..."

He glanced back at her, eyes crinkling at the corners. "Surprise."

"A plane? You weren't kidding about an adventure."

"I never kid," he said, pushing up the sleeves of his jacket. "Well, almost never."

He led her around the plane with a quiet reverence, his

hand skimming the edge of the wing. "It's a 1959 Cessna 172. She belonged to my grandfather. I've been restoring her for years. Had her flown from California and I've been taking her out on occasion in secret. Figured it was time to take her up again—and I wanted to share the flight with you."

Charlie Grace stared at the plane, emotions rising like tidewater. She hadn't expected this. Hadn't expected him to remember the offhand comment she'd made weeks ago about wondering what the Tetons looked like from a bird's eye view.

He opened the passenger-side door and offered his hand. "Come on, cowgirl. Let's go see your mountains."

The cockpit was small and smelled faintly of aged leather, oil, and the subtle tang of metal warmed by the sun. She settled into the seat, strapping in as Nick climbed in beside her, adjusting the dials with a calm competence that settled something inside her she hadn't even realized was frayed.

He handed her a headset. "You'll want this once we're in the air. It's noisy."

She put it on, her pulse drumming in her ears—not from fear, but from the swell of anticipation. The canopy of trees seemed to bow low around them, holding its breath.

Nick looked over at her. "Ready?"

She nodded.

The propeller whirred to life with a shuddering growl that quickly smoothed into a steady, throaty purr. Nick's hands moved with confidence—throttle, yoke, foot pedals—all second nature. As they taxied forward, her heart thudded in sync with the hum of the engine.

And then, the wheels lifted.

They were flying.

The air beneath them cradled the plane like invisible silk. Below, the valley surrounding Jackson Hole unrolled like a living map—rivers glinting in the morning sun, aspen groves flashing golden leaves, and soon she spotted her Teton Trails

Ranch, a patchwork of fences and pasture that made her heart twist with affection.

As they climbed, the Tetons rose to meet them—knife-edged and majestic, snow dusting the highest peaks signaling fall's advance. The sky above was a perfect western blue, clear and endless.

Nick's voice crackled in her headset. "That's Grand Teton coming up off the right wing."

She turned her head and gasped. The mountain towered above the range, proud and solemn, its glacier-scored face catching the light in angles of silver and stone.

"It's like looking into a bit of heaven placed on earth," she said softly.

"Exactly," he replied.

They soared past Cascade Canyon, its deep V carved into the range like a secret. Below, Jenny Lake mirrored the sky, cupped gently in the cradle of ancient rock.

The world fell away.

She forgot the guest ranch. The endless list of to-dos. The worry about her father's health. Even the lingering need to fix things—horses, broken fences, jammed camera shutters—but her truest habit was mending the people she loved, stitching up their heartaches with steady hands and never once asking who would mend hers.

Up here, there was only wind, sun, sky—and Nick.

She glanced over at him. He wasn't watching the mountains. He was watching her.

Her breath caught.

"What?" she asked, her voice barely audible even through the headset.

Nick's mouth curved just slightly. "Just wanted to see that look on your face."

She looked away, blinking fast. Could it be that sometimes you find your true direction reflected in someone else's eyes?

They flew for nearly an hour, tracing the spine of the range, dipping slightly to circle over the Snake River where a herd of elk meandered like slow-moving shadows in the morning light. The air grew cooler as they climbed higher, and she caught the faint smell of pine resin on the breeze creeping through a vent.

Finally, Nick turned the plane gently east, toward a remote valley dotted with lodgepole and a grassy landing strip near an alpine lake. He brought them down with smooth precision, the tires touching the ground with barely a bump.

She exhaled only then, realizing how long she'd been holding her breath.

Nick climbed out and opened her door. "Come on," he said, offering a hand. "I packed lunch."

The sun had climbed high by now, and the scent of wild sage mingled with damp earth. Birds called from the trees. A chipmunk darted across their path as they walked to a shady spot near the lake's edge, where Nick had already set out a blanket, a basket, and—of course—a thermos of coffee.

"You really thought of everything," she said, sitting cross-legged on the blanket.

"I thought of you," he said, handing her a sandwich.

They ate in quiet for a while, watching the sunlight dance on the ripples of the water. A butterfly landed on the corner of the blanket and stayed a while, flapping its wings like it had nowhere better to be.

After a long pause, Nick said, "You don't always have to carry everything, you know. You can put it down sometimes."

She looked at him, startled.

"I mean it," he continued. "You take care of everybody, Charlie Grace. But it's okay to let someone take care of you."

She couldn't speak for a moment.

"I don't know how to," she admitted.

Nick reached for her hand, his voice low. "Then let me be the one who helps."

Her heart twisted at that—and in the stillness of the mountains, in the hush that followed, she realized something. She felt light. Not just lighter. But free.

Not because her problems were gone. But because someone was quietly willing to hold the weight with her.

21

The call came just after dawn, the soft trill of her phone slicing through the quiet house like a blade. One look at the screen, and Reva knew before she answered.

Kellen sat up in the bed beside her, rubbing his face as she pressed the phone to her ear. A long pause. Then her mother's broken voice: "Ree-Ree…she's gone."

The words landed with the weight of a boulder on her chest. Though she'd known this moment was coming—had braced herself for it—grief hit with a force that buckled her soul. Reva curled into herself, the sobs tearing free in ragged waves, while Kellen gathered her close, rocking her like he would a wounded child.

Time blurred after that.

They packed in a haze of lists and whispered reminders. Dark dresses. Black suits. Little Lucan's tiny loafers. Tickets were booked, the car loaded. At the airport, Reva kept sunglasses pressed to her face to hide swollen eyes, the world moving around her in muffled tones as if she were underwater.

The flight was long, the air dry and stale. Reva sat stiff and silent, fingers clutched around a crumpled tissue, Kellen's steady hand resting over hers the whole way.

By the time they arrived in Georgia, the humid air wrapped around them like a heavy quilt. They drove straight to the old family homestead first, the pecan trees whispering in the breeze, Grand Memaw's absence as loud as a thunderclap in the silence.

The moment Reva stepped through the double doors of Grand Memaw's house, the weight of her loss was met with something even heavier—her memories.

As a little girl, Reva had wandered these wide halls in patent leather shoes, her fingers brushing the toile drapes and polished banisters, feeling like royalty in a house that always smelled faintly of roses. Every corner held hints of her past—Sunday dinners in the formal dining room, summers spent shelling pecans on the breezy back porch, nights curled up by the marble fireplace listening to Grand Memaw's stories about the land and the people who had built it.

This wasn't just a home—it was a southern treasure, polished and preserved with the kind of care born from pride and tradition. The wide foyer welcomed with its gleaming inlaid floors, a grand chandelier sparkling above like a crown of light. To the left, the formal parlor stood as pristine as ever, with its velvet-upholstered settee, carved tables, and a piano that hadn't been played in years but stood at attention all the same. Floral arrangements—fresh white gardenias and sky-blue hyacinths, of course—had been delivered and placed around the room, a nod to the woman who made hospitality an art form.

Her mother met her near the staircase, arms crossed tightly, her expression barely holding together. "She went peacefully, baby," she said softly, her voice catching. "Didn't suffer. Just... slipped away in her sleep."

Reva closed her eyes, tears rising fast. "That's something, at least," she whispered.

Her mama gently lifted Lucan from Reva's arms, cuddling him close and cooing soft, soothing words against his curls before turning to Kellen with a tearful smile and pulling him into a warm embrace.

They stood in silence for a moment before her mother cleared her throat and gestured toward the study. "There's something you should see. We found a quitclaim deed in her desk. Everything—this house, the farm, the operation—it's been left solely to you."

Reva's breath caught. "To me?" she said, barely above a whisper. "What about the boys?"

Her mother didn't flinch. "Your brothers are two halves of a broken compass—Quincy, always pushing forward with investments that are often unsound, and Mason, spinning quietly in place, unsure of where he belongs except for his music. Your grandmother knew what she was doing." Then, more gently, "She left trust funds for them. But she wanted Sunnyside Acres to go to the one person she trusted would carry it forward."

Reva wasn't naïve—she suspected her mother had a hand in all this, pushing Grand Memaw toward a decision that might bring her only daughter back home. She turned toward the office, the old door slightly ajar, the scent of lemon polish and old paper drifting out like an invitation.

She wasn't sure what her future looked like, but standing in that beautiful old house, hearing the truth wrapped in her mother's quiet resolve, she realized the decision she'd made to come home, though painful—was the right one.

THE DAY of the funeral dawned sticky and gray, as if even the heavens mourned.

The First Baptist Church—an imposing white-columned building with a steeple that scraped the sky—was already brimming by the time Reva stepped out of the car. She drew a deep breath, appreciating the scent of magnolias and star jasmine as she and Kellen moved for the wide portico, where townsfolk fanned themselves with folded bulletins, murmuring in low, respectful voices.

Inside, the wooden pews groaned under the sheer number of people. Rosetta Nygard had touched every life in this town it seemed—students she taught in Sunday school, neighbors she nursed through sickness, friends she cooked for when hard times hit. There wasn't an empty seat to be found.

Gospel music floated from the organ loft, swelling and breaking like the tide. Hymns that Grand Memaw had loved poured out, every note a fresh tear in Reva's heart.

Reva sat in the front row, flanked by her family. Her mother, regal even in bereavement, dabbed at her eyes with a lace handkerchief. Kellen, stone-faced, kept one protective arm around her. Her two brothers—Quincy in a crisp navy suit, every inch the businessman he aspired to be, and Mason, awkward in a jacket slightly too large—shifted uncomfortably in the pews, sadness etching their faces.

Kellen reached for her hand, his thumb tracing slow, soothing circles. But Reva felt barely tethered, her heartache so vast it threatened to pull her under completely.

When the pastor rose to speak—recounting Grand Memaw's strength, her stubborn faith, her fierce, abiding love for family—Reva bowed her head, hot tears spilling onto the stiff black fabric of her dress.

Eventually, the final hymn swelled through the sanctuary, the organ's rich notes trembling in the heavy air. As the last amen was spoken and the congregation rose to their feet, Reva stood too, feeling the hollow ache in her chest deepen. She turned to gather herself—and that's when she saw them.

Standing quietly at the back of the church, hands clasped, faces full of love, were Charlie Grace, Lila, and Capri.

Reva's breath caught, a fresh sob clawing its way up as she made her way to them. "What...what are you doing here?" she managed to croak.

Charlie Grace smiled first, her eyes glistening. "Real friends show up. No invitations needed."

Lila stepped forward, voice thick with emotion. "You've carried us through plenty, Reva. Now it's our turn."

Capri, normally the boldest, blinked fast against tears. "Yeah, you didn't think we'd let you face this without backup, did you?"

The dam inside Reva broke wide open. She surged forward, half-stumbling down the remaining aisle, and into their arms. They folded around her without hesitation, a fortress of friendship, of love.

The heartache of this loss had altered the shape of her life, but it hadn't stolen everything. People remained who mattered, and they were still here—in the hands that reached for her, the voices that called her name, the quiet certainty that she was loved beyond measure.

22

Reva crossed the sidewalk toward Town Hall, her lunch bag bumping gently against her hip. The morning sun glinted off the courthouse windows, casting long shadows across the square. She paused at the entrance, her hand resting on the worn brass handle, and let her gaze sweep over the familiar scene—the park benches, the lampposts, the steady rhythm of small-town life. It should have comforted her. Instead, her chest tightened with a hollow ache, a silent reminder of how much she loved it here.

Memaw was gone.

The farm would be hers.

Her future—Lucan's future—would soon take root in red clay soil, not the craggy Tetons she adored.

But not yet.

Not today.

Today she was still the mayor of Thunder Mountain, with work to do. Important work. Hard work.

Squaring her shoulders, Reva stepped into the crisp fall air, the familiar smell of brewing coffee and wet pine rising from the street. She bounded up the steps, and as she pushed through the heavy oak doors, Verna Billingsley was waiting—armed and ready.

"Good morning, Mayor Nygard," Verna chirped, her lipstick bright enough to stop traffic. She shoved a thick stack of papers into Reva's hands before she'd even made it past the reception desk.

Reva blinked. "What in the world is this?"

Verna sniffed primly. "Applications."

"Applications?" Reva repeated. She flipped through the sheaf—cover letters, résumés, even a few headshots. "We haven't even posted the sheriff's job yet."

Verna's mouth curved in a smug little smile. "This is Thunder Mountain, ma'am. You think you have to post something for folks to know the position is up for grabs?"

Reva sighed and tucked the papers under her arm, heading for her office. "I was hoping to have at least five minutes to get settled."

Verna trailed behind, clipboard in hand. "Well, make it quick. Ernie Dupree's already called twice to say he's 'highly interested' in the position. So has Midge Cartwright—and I'm pretty sure she's never even fired a squirt gun."

Reva pushed open the door to her office and paused, taking a steadying breath. Sunlight slanted across her desk, illuminating the framed photo of Kellen and Lucan she'd placed beside the phone. A tiny lump rose in her throat, but she forced it down.

So many changes ahead.

She crossed the room and set the applications down with a thump. "Let's start a list of serious candidates. People with actual law enforcement experience. And give preference to local."

The town could weather a lot—harsh winters, tourist swarms, even the occasional tremor—but its sheriff had to be one of their own, someone who understood the unspoken codes of Thunder Mountain, where trust wasn't given lightly, and respect was earned over coffee counters and cattle gates.

Verna scribbled something on her clipboard, mumbling under her breath.

"What was that?" Reva asked, cocking a brow.

Verna looked up, deadpan. "I said that rules out three-quarters of these applicants—or more."

Despite herself, Reva chuckled—a real, honest-to-goodness laugh. It felt foreign in her chest, like something she'd forgotten how to do.

"Thanks, Verna," she said, softer now. "For holding down the fort while I was gone."

Verna's face softened, too. "I've got you, Mayor. Whatever you need."

Reva nodded, a tightness building behind her eyes. She glanced at the mountain of applications and then at the phone already blinking with messages.

"Okay," she told herself, straightening a stack of papers. "Time to get to work."

Reva had been at it for hours, her eyes blurring from scanning Verna's list and the résumés, frustrated at the lack of qualified candidates, when a sharp rap sounded at her office door. She rubbed her temples and looked up, surprised to see Gibbs Nichols standing in the doorway, hat in hand.

"Sorry to barge in," he said, his voice more serious than usual. "Verna wasn't at her desk."

Reva glanced at the clock on her computer. "She must be at lunch," she murmured, setting down her pen.

Gibbs stepped in, a little awkward, the toes of his boots scuffing against the rug. He didn't sit, just twisted his hat between his hands.

"I know you're busy, Reva," he began, clearing his throat. "But I'm here because I want to throw my name in the hat for sheriff."

Reva leaned back slowly, folding her hands over her stomach. Of all the candidates she'd imagined, Gibbs Nichols hadn't been high on the list.

He must've read the skepticism on her face because he hurried on.

"Look, I know I've been a screw-up in a lot of ways. Everybody in this town knows it, no point pretending otherwise. But that's behind me. It's different now." His gaze was steady, and for once, free of the old defensiveness. "I'm a husband now. A faithful spouse," he added pointedly. "And a father—not just to Jewel, but to the new little one. I need to support them, Reva. Not just with a paycheck, but with something that matters. Something that tells Jewel that people can change. That you can fall down and still stand back up."

He paused, taking a breath. "I know this town. I know its people, its back roads, its history. I know who's got a short fuse and who just needs someone to listen. Fleet taught me more than folks realize—about patience, about reading between the lines. About not making a bad situation worse just because you can."

Reva stayed silent, studying him. He was older now, a little thicker around the middle, a few more creases around the eyes. But there was a steadiness in his posture she hadn't seen before.

Gibbs shifted and glanced at the leaning stack of applications on her desk.

"All I'm asking is that you consider it," he said quietly. "Not for who I used to be, but for who I am now."

He squared his shoulders, set his hat back on his head, and gave her a nod. "Thank you, Mayor."

Without waiting for a reply, he turned and walked out, the door clicking shut behind him.

Reva sat still for a long moment, the clock ticking softly in the background.

The office felt heavier after Gibbs left, like the very air had thickened. Reva leaned back in her chair, staring at the door as if she could still see him standing there.

Hiring a sheriff wasn't just about filling a vacancy. It wasn't even just about safety. It was about trust. About the soul of the town.

She tapped her pen against the desk, staring at the stack of applications. There were others, sure—a few with impressive credentials, a couple of retired lawmen from as far away as Montana and Idaho, looking for one last quiet post before the rocking chair.

They didn't know who still left their back doors unlocked out of habit.

They didn't know that you didn't write up a citation when Harold Riggins's cows wandered Main Street—you just helped herd them back behind the sagging fence.

They didn't know the difference between good trouble and bad trouble.

And yet...

Her mind flickered to all the times Gibbs Nichols had let people down. The youthful recklessness. The broken promises. The hot temper that had once been a little too quick to spark. The pain he'd caused Charlie Grace...multiple times.

Could people really change?

Or did they just get better at hiding the parts of themselves that disappointed you?

She sighed, picking up a résumé from the pile, but her eyes didn't track the words. Her mind replayed the way Gibbs had stood there—no excuses, no swagger, just raw honesty.

And maybe, just maybe, that counted for more than a perfect record.

Reva leaned back again, the pen twirling slowly between her fingers. This wasn't a simple choice. It never was when it came to people you cared about.

But maybe, just maybe, the best leaders weren't the ones

with the cleanest pasts. Maybe they were the ones who knew how badly it hurt to fall—and how hard you had to fight to stand back up.

Another knock sounded again at her door, pulling her from her thoughts.

This time, she smiled wryly.

News sure did travel fast in Thunder Mountain.

23

Two days later, Reva sat behind the wheel of her SUV in the Moose Chapel parking lot, fingers curled around the steering wheel. The evening air was crisp, her breath ghosting lightly on the windshield as she exhaled. She hadn't even turned on the engine.

Inside the church, the folding chairs were already stacked, the coffee urn scrubbed clean, the faint echoes of murmured prayers and clinking mugs still fresh in her mind. Tonight's AA meeting had been different. Raw. She had stood and said words she hadn't uttered in years—not even to Kellen.

"I made a big decision that is going to affect me and those I love in profound ways. I'm scared. Not that I made the wrong decision, but that I'm not strong enough for what comes next. And I can't fix this by working harder, planning better, or pretending I'm more resilient than I am."

The room had nodded with a kind of sacred understanding, but now that she was alone, the vulnerability pressed heavier on her chest than any mountain.

Her phone buzzed against the console.

A group text.

Lila: *"Rustic Pine. Tonight."*

Capri: *"No arguments, Nygard. We know you're busy. But it's been nearly three weeks."*

Charlie Grace: *"We're ordering your favorite burger. So, no excuses."*

A laugh—sharp and unexpected—bubbled out of Reva's throat. Guilty as charged. She had been a bit distant since returning from Georgia, and on purpose. No one knew her better, and she simply wasn't ready to risk having to tell them. Not yet. But leave it to her girlfriends to know when she needed some fun.

She wiped at her eyes with the sleeve of her jacket and put the car into gear.

The Rustic Pine's weathered sign swung lightly in the breeze as Reva pulled into a vacant parking spot. Through the wide front windows, she spotted them immediately—her girls—huddled in their favorite corner booth. A candle flickered between them, catching the glint of Capri's earrings and Charlie Grace's tumbling curls.

Reva hesitated on the sidewalk, suddenly unsure if she could handle this tonight—the looks in their eyes, the tenderness she wasn't sure she deserved. But then Lila caught her gaze through the window, smiled softly, and mouthed, "Come on."

Taking a deep breath, she exited her vehicle and made her way to the entrance.

She pushed through the door, the warm rush of old wood and laughter enveloping her like a blanket. Annie Cumberland stopped polishing some glasses and waved from behind the bar. Someone—probably Nicola Cavendish—was butchering karaoke in the back room. All of it so achingly familiar.

"Hey, stranger," Capri called, sliding over to make room.

Charlie Grace patted the chair beside her. "Look at you, showing up late and still scoring the best seat."

Reva sank into the offered seat, the weight of their welcome undoing something brittle inside her. Before she could say a word, Lila reached across the table and set a thick, dripping cheeseburger in front of her, complete with onion rings stacked like a crown.

"We've missed you," Lila said simply.

Reva picked up the burger with shaky hands and took a bite, the smoky flavor exploding across her tongue. Goodness, she hadn't realized how hungry she was.

They let her eat in peace, chatting about everything and nothing—like Nicola Cavendish's latest mishap when her Yorkie helped herself to the dessert table at the library luncheon, Bodhi West's latest rafting mishap, the Knit Wit ladies scheming to get Fleet Southcott a retirement party he swore he didn't want.

But eventually, the conversation circled back, like a river curving toward the sea, inevitable. They sat in companionable silence for several seconds before Charlie Grace cupped her hand around her beer mug and leaned forward. "When were you going to tell us?"

Reva blinked, caught off guard.

How did they already know?

Reva swallowed, wiped her mouth, and set the burger down. "I wasn't sure. I guess...I was hoping the decision would somehow make itself."

Capri arched an eyebrow. "And here I thought you were allergic to indecision."

That pulled a nervous chuckle from Reva. She looked around at their faces, all so dear, so deeply etched into the story of her life. How could she find the words?

"We know something is up with you." Lila glanced between the others for confirmation. "We can tell."

"And it's more than your Grand Memaw...or needing to replace Fleet," suggested Charlie Grace. "Are we right?"

Reva pressed her palms against the table to steady herself.

"Kellen and I are moving to Georgia," she said finally. "Lucan needs deep family roots—the kind I was grounded in. And my Grand Memaw left me Sunnyside Acres." Her voice cracked. "She trusted me to carry our family's heritage forward."

For a moment, no one spoke. The weight of Reva's news settled over them, heavy and sharp. Charlie Grace was the first to move, reaching across the table to squeeze Reva's hand, her eyes glassy with emotion.

Lila swallowed hard and offered a tremulous smile. "If it's what you have to do, we'll stand behind you. Every step."

Capri, usually the boldest, leaned back in her chair, blinking fast. "We're losing a piece of us," she said quietly. "But we're not losing you. Don't you ever think that."

Around the table, heads nodded. The bond between them might stretch across states, but it wouldn't break.

"Thunder Mountain without you?" Capri added, her voice unusually soft. "That's like a river with no water."

Lila blinked fast, trying and failing to keep the tears at bay. "You're this town's anchor, Reva. And ours. Always have been."

Reva rubbed her temple. "I'm not sure I even know how to leave. I don't know who I am without...this."

Charlie Grace smiled through her tears. "You're still you. You're simply planting new seeds somewhere else."

"And anyway," Capri added, tossing a cocktail napkin at her. "Don't think for a second you're escaping us. We'll show up in Georgia uninvited with casseroles and lawn chairs if we have to."

Reva laughed, the sound rich and a little wobbly.

Annie dropped off a tray of milkshakes without asking, her slight smile threaded with compassion. "On the house," she said before retreating to the table next to them.

"You know what this means," Capri said, leaning in conspiratorially. "You're getting a going-away party whether you want it or not."

"Biggest shindig since Verna Billingsley's ill-advised llama festival," Charlie Grace added.

Reva shook her head, but her heart soaked it in—all of it.

"Life pulls us in different directions," Lila said with a soft smile. "But love...love keeps the roots alive no matter how far you go."

The words found a place deep inside Reva's chest, settling there like an ember catching flame.

Later, after the milkshakes were drained and the last of the fries had been picked at, they lingered in the parking lot under a sky smeared with stars.

The wind stirred Reva's hair, carrying the sharp sweetness of evening. She tucked her hands into her jacket pockets, reluctant to end the night.

Capri slung an arm around her shoulders. "You're not losing us," she said fiercely. "We're stitched into your story. Permanently."

Charlie Grace held up her phone. "Group text stays active. No excuses. Weekly updates. Pictures mandatory."

"And Zoom calls," added Lila.

"With margaritas in hand," Capri offered. "And lemonade for you."

They laughed, they cried, they promised.

And Reva, standing under the faded glow of the streetlamp with her forever friends beside her, realized something true.

Distance changes a lot of things—routines, conversations, the small, easy moments you take for granted. But real friendship—the kind built from years of laughter, heartache, and everything in between—doesn't unravel just because the map says you're far apart.

That kind of friendship just stretches...and somehow, it holds.

At least she hoped so.

24

By Monday morning, news traveled like wildfire through Thunder Mountain. Mayor Reva Nygard was leaving.

Reva barely made it through the front doors of Town Hall without someone grabbing her elbow, pulling her in for a hug, or slipping her a note. She smiled until her cheeks ached. She blinked back tears so many times her eyes burned.

By noon, her assistant Verna Billingsley appeared in the doorway of her office, looking both frantic and delighted.

"I've already planned a going-away parade," Verna said, waving a clipboard as if it were a royal decree. "We'll need floats. Banners. Balloons. I'm thinking a pie contest, too. Maybe a cowbell-off!"

Reva stared at her, dumbfounded. "A cowbell-off?"

Verna nodded vigorously. "It's where everyone brings their loudest cowbell and competes for the title of Thunder Mountain's Noisiest Neighbor."

"I...don't think we need—"

"It's already on the flyer!" Verna chirped, turning on her heel and disappearing down the hallway. "Besides, this is a big one. A double celebration. Thunder Mountain is losing both you and our beloved Fleet. We can't let this sad milestone pass without proper recognition."

Reva dropped her forehead into her hands and groaned. But under the groan was a smile she couldn't quite suppress.

Thunder Mountain loved its own fiercely—and sometimes absurdly.

The rest of the day passed in a haze of handshakes, hugs, and familiar faces.

Oma dropped by with a Tupperware container of warm cinnamon rolls, the smell sweet and buttery. She patted Reva's cheek, leaving a dusting of flour on her skin.

Later, Pastor Pete stopped by, carrying a worn Bible tucked under one arm.

"I know you're following what your heart tells you," he said, his voice thick. "But don't you forget—you've got two homes now. Here and there."

Even Nicola Cavendish popped her head into Reva's office with a sniffle.

"You're leaving a mark on this town no earthquake could shake loose," she said, dabbing at her eyes with a monogrammed handkerchief. Her tiny dog, Sweetpea, yapped in agreement from her designer purse.

Reva smiled and thanked her, feeling the layers of her life here wrap around her heart tighter with each farewell.

In the late afternoon, Reva drove down the street to the sheriff's department.

Fleet Southcott was already waiting on the front steps, his posture a little more stooped than usual, his badge polished until it caught the sun. He held a battered clipboard in one hand.

"Got your recommendation for the council," Fleet said, handing over the clipboard. "Gibbs Nichols. Kid's got spirit."

Reva accepted his gesture, her throat tightening.

"You're a legend, Fleet," she said quietly. "Not easily replaced, my friend."

He chuckled, his gaze sweeping over the town. "Nah. Just an old man who loved his people."

"You kept us safe," Reva insisted. "You gave this town your heart."

"As did you, Mayor." Fleet's eyes softened. "Don't you go thinking you're not doing a big thing by moving down to Georgia, girl. It's gotta be hard on you. Just remember, home ain't a dot on a map. It's where you pour your love."

Fleet clapped her shoulder, firm and steady. He smiled, seeming to have made peace with the changes forced upon him. Reva took note, believing she needed to do the same.

She wanted to believe that letting go didn't have to feel so much like tearing herself in two.

Later that evening, after Lucan was tucked into bed and Kellen sat reviewing paperwork in the den, Reva stood barefoot on the back porch.

The mountains loomed in the distance, dark and steady.

She drew a deep breath.

Thunder Mountain would be here long after she was gone. Its ridges and valleys, its storms and clearings, would hold pieces of her soul forever.

She hugged her sweater closer and let herself feel it—the ache, the gratitude, the hope. She wasn't just leaving a town. She was leaving a piece of herself behind. And in exchange, she was carrying all of this love into the next chapter.

Kellen was suddenly by her side. He placed both his hands on her shoulders, whispered into her hair, "Everything's going to be all right, babe. Rarely does life stay the same. But we'll be doing this together."

She nodded, turned, and buried her face against his chest.

Yes, her husband was right.

We thought change was the enemy—that if we just held

still long enough, maybe life wouldn't find us. But life always found us. It shoved us forward, ready or not.

IN THE DAYS following Reva's announcement, the weight of the news continued to press heavy on her girlfriends. It wasn't just what she said—it was everything it meant.

Charlie Grace busied herself with ranch chores she didn't really need to do, trying to outrun the feeling that something was slipping away.

Capri threw herself into work too, but even the river, wild and restless like her, couldn't carry away the quiet grief pooling inside her.

Lila sat on the clinic porch at sunset, coffee cooling in her hands, staring at the hills where their futures had once seemed so certain.

They didn't talk about it, not yet. Maybe they didn't know how. All they knew was that something had shifted, and no matter how hard they tried to hold it together, the cracks were already showing.

Hearing Reva's plans left her friends gutted in a way none of them wanted to admit aloud. They had weathered boyfriends, marriages, deaths, and births together—standing shoulder to shoulder through everything life threw their way.

But this? This was different. This was a goodbye written in slow, heavy strokes.

Love made you brave. But losing someone you loved—even when it was the right thing—made you fragile in ways you never expected.

25

Capri stood barefoot in the middle of her kitchen, wiping down an already spotless counter. The late afternoon sun slanted through the new windows Jake had installed, bathing the space in a golden warmth that hadn't existed before the renovation. Everything gleamed—the new cabinets Jake had installed, the creamy stone countertops, and the fresh blue of the backsplash gave the room a brightness that whispered *new beginnings*.

The old kitchen had been dark and cramped, a place that felt stuck in another time. This one? This one felt open, alive—like maybe change wasn't the enemy she'd spent years believing it was.

"You know they're just coming for food, right?" Jake's voice floated in from the mudroom, thick with amusement. "Not to pass a white glove inspection."

Capri turned to find him leaning against the doorframe, arms crossed over his chest, watching her with a lazy grin that threatened to unravel her whole fake sense of calm.

"I'm setting the tone," she said primly, grabbing a dish towel and giving the counter a final swipe. "This is a classy operation."

Jake laughed. "You made deviled eggs and opened a bag of chips. If that's your idea of classy, babe, you're about to set a new low."

"Excuse me," she sniffed, flicking the towel at him. "I plated the chips."

Jake ducked the flying dish towel with a chuckle, then crossed the room, slow and easy. He glanced around, his gaze lingering on the blue tile backsplash, the open shelving with her mismatched mugs, the sunlight pouring across the wide farmhouse sink. "We did good with this place," he said, softer now. "Really good."

Something caught in her throat at the warmth in his voice. She made a joke of it, bumping her hip into his. "Guess I'm not allergic to change after all."

"Good," Jake murmured, close enough that she could smell the hint of soap and sawdust clinging to his shirt. "Because you're about to have a houseful of it."

As if on cue, tires crunched outside and a familiar chorus of voices rose—the guys, loud and laughing already. Capri felt a surge of nerves and excitement at once. This wasn't just another dinner. It was a new kind of memory being stitched together.

"Brace yourself," she said, shooting Jake a grin as she headed for the door. "They're going to eat everything that's not nailed down."

"They'll bring more food. You wait and see," Jake called after her, chuckling as the first knock rattled the door.

Capri yanked the door open just as Kellen, Nick, and Reva came up the steps, arms full of covered dishes and six-packs. Whit, Lila, and Charlie Grace were pulling things from their cars.

"Smells good in there!" Kellen boomed, holding up a foil-wrapped tray like it was a trophy. "Hope you made extra, Cap. I brought my appetite."

"You always bring your appetite," Reva said dryly, elbowing him as she squeezed past. She carried a big salad bowl cradled against her hip and a bottle of sparkling cider tucked under one arm. "It's his spiritual gift."

Jake leaned down and stage-whispered in Capri's ear, "Told you they'd bring reinforcements."

Whit came in last, balancing a pie box precariously in one hand and tipping an invisible hat with the other. "Hope everyone is ready for a night of far too much food."

"Isn't that the theme of every time we get together?" Capri quipped, grabbing the pie before Whit could drop it.

"Hey, hey, careful!" Whit said, pretending to clutch his chest. "That's homemade."

"Store-bought homemade," Lila chimed in, arriving right behind him with Charlie Grace. "We all saw you sneaking out of the bakery this afternoon."

Capri, missing none of the banter, wrinkled her nose. "That's cheating, Whit."

Whit held up three fingers solemnly. "In my defense, it's from the good bakery. You won't even taste the shame."

Everyone laughed, the kind of easy, full-bellied sound Capri realized she cherished more than she cared to admit.

Within minutes, the house filled with the clatter of dishes being set down, chairs scraping, the low thrum of old country music playing on Jake's Bluetooth speaker. Capri's kitchen—her new kitchen—hummed with life, the way she'd always dreamed it would.

Jake slid a platter of ribs onto the center island and shot her a wink. "Operation Mood Lift, officially underway."

Capri smiled, a real one this time, feeling the energy spark around her. They couldn't erase the hard things. But maybe, for tonight, they could outshine them.

They piled their plates high—ribs, deviled eggs, potato salad, cornbread muffins still warm from the oven—and squeezed around Capri's refurbished farmhouse table. Capri ended up wedged between Jake and Charlie Grace, with Nick perched on a stool nearby, already buttering a second muffin with alarming precision.

"So," Whit said around a mouthful of ribs. "This whole Georgia thing. How soon are you two planning the big move?"

Reva dabbed her mouth with a napkin, her smile steady even if her eyes flickered just the tiniest bit. "As soon as we can get everything wrapped up here. There's a lot to do."

Jake set down his fork. "Been there, done that. It's a lot."

Reva ticked off the list on her fingers. "Yeah—for starters, I have to hire Fleet's replacement. The town can't exactly run without a sheriff. I'm not leaving until we find a suitable candidate and get him or her sworn in."

Nick leaned forward, interest sparking. "Are you going to open it up to the public?"

"Already did," Reva said, her tone brisk. Then she glanced across the table, locking eyes with Charlie Grace. "But truth is, I'm thinking of offering it to Gibbs."

The table went quiet for a half-second longer than comfortable. Capri shifted in her seat, ready to step in if needed, but Charlie Grace only lifted her wine glass with calm grace.

"I hope it's the break he needs," Charlie Grace said, her voice even. "I've seen a lot of change in him lately. And he does love this town."

A low current of respect moved through the table. Capri felt it in the slight nod Jake gave, the way Kellen let out a quiet *hmm* of agreement.

"And me," Reva said lightly. "Well, I'm going to have the impossible task of finding a new candidate for mayor."

"Easier said than done," Capri said, pointing her fork at Reva. "You're irreplaceable."

"Absolutely," Lila added. "We should just retire the office after you leave."

Reva shook her head, smiling. "Nobody's irreplaceable. Not even me. City Council will handle the election, and Thunder Mountain will have a new mayor before you know it. The right person will step up. That's how this works."

The girls exchanged doubtful looks but said nothing, the truth too heavy to argue with.

Across the table, Kellen reached for Reva's hand. "We've already hired a moving company," he said, brightening the mood. "Full service. They pack, haul, even unpack if we want."

"Sounds like a good plan," Jake said. "If you need extra hands, you know where to find us."

"Same here," Nick added. "You just say the word."

Reva's face softened, the mask of professionalism slipping just enough to show the gratitude underneath. "I don't know how we're going to say goodbye," she admitted. "But knowing everyone is rooting for us...makes it a whole lot easier."

Capri poured herself another glass of wine. "What about the house?"

Kellen and Reva exchanged glances. "We're keeping it. For now," Reva said.

"We both like the idea of having a vacation home in the mountains." He turned to his wife. "And we *are* going to take vacations, right?"

Reva grinned and bumped his shoulder with her own. "No doubt I can be talked into visits to Thunder Mountain every summer."

The table laughed.

Capri felt a swell of something deeper—pride, love, a stubborn kind of hope. She raised her glass, catching Jake's eye as she did.

"To new adventures," Capri echoed, her voice sure and

steady. "And to knowing Reva and Kellen will always have a place to come back to."

Glasses clinked.

Then, with a crooked grin, she added, "And, if the world's going to turn upside down, at least we remembered to bring good food and wine."

26

Reva adjusted the strap of her purse as she stepped up onto the Nichols' sagging front porch, the wood creaking under her boots. A faded welcome mat that read *Bless This Mess* made her smile. Somehow, it felt like the Nichols household had summed up small-town life in three little words.

She rapped her knuckles against the screen door. Inside, the television blared.

After a minute, Gibbs appeared, wrestling a squirming one-year-old perched on his hip. He cracked open the door, flushed and winded. "Hey, Mayor. This is a surprise. Come on in, if you dare."

"Perhaps I should have called first," Reva commented. In her haste to deliver news of her decision, she'd skipped her normal manners.

"No, not at all. Come on in." He waved her inside.

The small house was pure chaos. Toys littered the worn hardwood floor—plastic blocks, stuffed animals, a rubber chicken with one leg missing. The air smelled faintly of vanilla from a candle battling against the scent of last night's spaghetti.

Lizzy, Gibbs' young wife, shot up from the couch, shoving aside a laundry basket overflowing with onesies and tiny socks.

"Sorry 'bout the mess," Gibbs said, setting the toddler down. Immediately, the little boy crawled and made a beeline for a toy drum, whacking it with enthusiastic fists.

"Don't worry," Reva said, smiling warmly. "I'm not here to judge your housekeeping skills."

Gibbs grabbed the remote and muted the television. The sudden quiet felt heavy. He motioned for Reva to sit, clearing a toy truck off the armchair. Lizzy hovered nearby, her face a mixture of curiosity and nerves.

Reva leaned forward, elbows on her knees. "Gibbs, I'm here because I have made a decision about the sheriff's position."

Gibbs face immediately filled with disappointment. "I understand."

Reva shook her head. "It's not what you're thinking. After a lot of thought—and some prayer—I'd like to officially offer you the position of Sheriff of Thunder Mountain."

Gibbs' jaw slackened. Lizzy gasped softly and pressed a hand to her mouth. The baby thudded his drumstick on the floor, oblivious.

"You're serious?" Gibbs said, voice rough.

"As serious as it gets," Reva replied. "This isn't just a badge and a title. It's a trust. The whole town will be depending on you, Gibbs. To keep them safe, yes—but also to be reliable, and never to let them down. Fair. Steady. Strong, even when things get tough."

Reva looked him directly in the eyes. "Do you understand, Gibbs?"

Gibbs' eyes shone as he nodded slowly, almost like he didn't trust himself to speak yet.

"I'll expect you to attend additional training. You'll work closely with the council. You'll need to build bridges, not walls. And you have to live like every kid out there is watching you—

because they are. No more..." She paused, searching for the right words. "Misdeeds," she finally said.

He swallowed hard, glancing at Lizzy, who was now openly crying. She crossed to him and grabbed his hand.

"I won't let you down, Mayor," he promised.

"You may have heard," Reva added gently. "Hiring you will be one of my last official acts as mayor."

Lizzy's head jerked up. "You're quitting?" she whispered.

Reva gave a small nod, her throat tightening. "Not quitting. Leaving. Kellen and I are moving to Georgia soon. Family duties call."

Gibbs rubbed a hand over his short hair, stunned. "You're the heart of this town, Reva. Thunder Mountain simply won't be the same without you at the helm."

"I'm just one part of this community," she said, her voice steady. "It's your time now. Don't let them down."

He stood up straighter, still clutching Lizzy's hand. "I won't. I swear it."

The toddler, sensing the serious mood, waddled over and tugged at Reva's boot with a sticky hand. She laughed softly and reached down, ruffling the boy's blond hair.

"Looks like you've already got a good deputy," she said, straightening.

Gibbs chuckled, a little shaky. "Thank you for this chance, Reva. I'll make you proud."

"You already have," she said, glancing at his wife and son.

As she walked back out onto the porch, the door swinging shut behind her, Reva paused for a moment to take it all in—the chaos, the love, the hope. Thunder Mountain would be just fine.

She smiled, blinking against the sting in her eyes, and headed for her car.

27

Weeks had passed, but the quiet ache in Reva's heart hadn't dulled as Kellen pulled into the Community Center field. Cars lined both sides of the gravel drive, a few with their doors open wide like the arms of old friends. Kids darted between rows of folding tables, their hands and faces sticky with melting snow cones. A bluegrass band strummed near the old oak tree, the sharp twang of the banjo mixing with the distant clang of a cowbell somewhere out of sight.

Reva smiled despite the tight knot in her chest. Only in Thunder Mountain would a farewell party look more like a county fair.

Kellen parked his truck beneath a sprawling cottonwood, its leaves now golden. Lucan was out first, clutching a framed photograph they'd brought along—the one of Reva, Capri, Charlie Grace, and Lila as kids, sunburned and grinning with their arms slung around each other.

Lucan cradled the framed photo like it was treasure. "Don't worry, I'll keep it safe!" he said, puffing out his chest.

Reva tousled his curls, her heart squeezing. "I know you will, buddy."

She took a breath, feeling the familiar pinch behind her throat. Today was it. The official goodbye. No more stalling, no more pretending. By this time tomorrow, they'd be heading east toward Georgia—and toward a future she could barely bring herself to imagine.

As she stepped onto the grass, a sudden cheer broke out from the crowd. The whole town had shown up. Oma waved from near the pie table, a Tupperware container tucked under her arm. Pastor Pete and Annie Cumberland manned the grill, smoke rising as they flipped burgers with easy, practiced motions. The Knit Wit ladies bustled between tables, their colorful skirts flapping, balancing plates piled high with deviled eggs and potato salad. Of course, Nicola Cavendish had made it, her enormous sunhat casting shade over her little dog Sweetpea, nestled in a pink sling across her chest, while she handed out tiny American flags to whoever would take one.

"You didn't think we'd let you sneak out of town without a proper send-off, did you?" Annie hollered over the music.

Reva shook her head, her voice catching. "You are all something else."

"You're family," Oma said firmly, pressing a cinnamon roll into her hand. "And we take care of our own."

The air was thick with the smell of charcoal and baked peaches. Tables sagged under the weight of every comfort food imaginable—racks of ribs, piles of buttery cornbread, bowls of baked beans swimming with smoky bacon. Reva barely had time to set her plate down before the line of well-wishers started.

Pastor Pete gripped her hand. His voice was thick when he said, "Your faith helped build this town stronger than any ordinance ever could, Reva."

Albie Barton, the town newspaper editor, handed her a

framed front page. Big bold letters read: *FAREWELL, BUT NEVER FORGOTTEN.*

Fleet Southcott, his hands shaking slightly, pressed something into her palm. She opened it to find a battered antique deputy's badge.

"Just in case Georgia needs another sheriff," he said with a wink.

Reva glanced across the crowd to where Gibbs stood near the parking area, badge gleaming on his chest, arms folded as he scanned the crowd with quiet authority. He gave Reva a respectful nod—still getting used to the weight of the job but wearing it like he meant to earn it.

Each goodbye chipped away at her. But she smiled through it, her heart swelling and splintering all at once. This was love—the messy, generous, overwhelming kind. She had given her whole heart to Thunder Mountain, and the town had loved her right back.

She moved slowly through the crowd, pausing every few feet, not because she was being polite—but because she couldn't rush this. Every hand she shook, every back she patted, held a memory. The librarian who'd slipped books into Lucan's backpack without due dates. The rancher who once showed up in her driveway during a snowstorm with a cord of firewood and didn't ask a single question. The high school kid who'd nervously handed her a homemade flyer about starting a skate park and now stood beside her, six inches taller, holding his toddler.

Near the edge of the lawn, she caught sight of the old wooden community bulletin board, sun-faded and covered in layers of curling flyers—lost pets, bake sales, prayer meetings. She'd once taped her very first campaign flyer to that board, fingers shaking, heart pounding.

Now, a fresh sheet of paper had been pinned to the top: *"THANK YOU, REVA."* It was scrawled in a dozen different inks, covered in notes from townsfolk. She moved closer and scanned the words—some funny, some tear-stained. *You made Thunder Mountain feel safe. We'll miss you. Don't forget who you are, even if you live where sweet tea is served cold.*

Just then, Nicola Cavendish tottered over in a pair of heeled boots clearly not meant for grass. Sweetpea barked indignantly from her sling as Nicola thrust a small velvet pouch into Reva's hands.

"This is for you," Nicola said, her voice wobbling between theatrical and sincere. "It's a Saint Christopher medal. It belonged to Wooster's mother, and I've decided you're worthy of it."

Reva blinked. "Nicola...this is—"

"Don't make a fuss," Nicola interrupted, waving a bejeweled hand. "Just wear it and don't get too attached to those backroads of Georgia. And if you come home for a visit, bring a bag of those boiled peanuts I keep reading about," she said.

Reva was still laughing when she turned and nearly collided with Jewel, who looked like she'd been trying her best not to cry. The girl threw her arms around Reva's waist and held on tight.

"Are you really gonna go?" she whispered.

Reva crouched down so they were eye to eye. "I am, sweetheart. But guess what? You're coming with me."

Jewel's brows knit together. "I am?"

"In stories," Reva said, tapping Jewel's chest. "In the way I talk about you. In every memory I carry. That means you have to keep doing amazing things, so I always have new stories to tell."

Off to one side, Lucan had joined a circle of kids playing tag near the hay bales. His laughter rang out bright and unburdened. Kellen stood nearby, talking with Charlie Grace and Whit, his arms crossed but his smile easy. For a second, Reva let herself stop trying to memorize everything. She didn't need to.

The people she loved were not fading—they were anchoring her, steady as the Tetons.

Midway through the afternoon, Annie climbed up onto a small wooden stage and banged a cowbell above her head.

"Listen up, everyone!" she shouted, grinning. "We've got a few words before we let this woman escape!"

Capri and Jake nudged Reva forward. Capri leaned in and whispered, "Better get used to public adoration, Madame Mayor-for-Life."

Rolling her eyes, Reva made her way up to the stage, shielding her eyes from the bright sun overhead.

Pastor Pete was the first to take the microphone. His usual booming voice softened as he scanned the crowd.

"I could stand up here and list Reva Nygard's titles—attorney, mayor, advocate, friend. But titles don't tell the whole story," he said, pausing. "Reva didn't just serve this town. She mothered it. She fought for it. She loved it when it was messy and stubborn and broken down the middle. She taught us that real leadership isn't about power. It's about love."

He turned and smiled at her, his eyes shining.

"You're not just moving to Georgia, Reva. You're taking a part of us with you and planting a piece of Thunder Mountain there."

The crowd roared with applause. Kids whistled. Someone blew a kazoo off-key, and Reva laughed through the prickling behind her eyes.

Then Verna Billingsley bustled up to the stage, her tight bun wobbling as she adjusted her glasses with flair.

"I hereby declare," Verna announced dramatically. "That Reva Nygard shall henceforth and forevermore be known as Honorary Citizen of Thunder Mountain, with all privileges and pie discounts therein!"

She unfurled a glittery certificate and pinned a gold ribbon to Reva's shirt. The whole town burst out laughing.

"Pie discounts?" Reva said, clutching her sides. "Now that's a deal I'll take."

When the laughter faded, Reva stepped to the mic. For a moment, she couldn't speak. She looked out over the sea of faces—Capri, Charlie Grace blinking fast against tears, Lila holding tight to Whit's hand, Jewel twirling in circles near the bandstand.

She swallowed hard. How could she possibly say what this place had meant to her?

"I don't have a fancy speech," she said finally, her voice trembling. "How could I ever express what I'm feeling right now—what you all mean to me? And, how hard it is to say goodbye? All I have is a heart that's full to bursting. These many years in Thunder Mountain have been the pinnacle of my existence, the heartbeat of my soul."

She paused, steadying herself.

"This town, these mountains—all of you. You're stitched into me. I'm better because of you. And wherever I go, I'll carry you with me."

The silence that fell was thick and reverent, broken only by the soft clatter of a breeze shifting through the cottonwoods.

"Thank you," Reva finished simply. "Thank you for being my home. And we'll be back as often as we can visit. You can count on it!"

The crowd erupted again—cheering, clapping, stomping their feet in the grass.

And standing there in the warm sunlight, the laughter and music swirling all around her, Reva knew once again she wasn't leaving Thunder Mountain behind.

She was taking the town—these people—with her, tucked safely into every beat of her heart.

28

Morning light slanted through the wide windows of Reva's living room, illuminating the half-packed boxes stacked along the walls. The house, usually so full of life and laughter, felt strangely hollow, like a song winding to its final note.

Reva knelt by the couch, wrestling Lucan into his sneakers while he chattered nonstop about the adventure ahead.

"We're gonna see Grandma's big trees,' he said, swinging his legs. "And pecans! And armadillos!"

Reva smiled as she tied his laces. "That's right, baby. Lots of new things to see."

Kellen appeared in the doorway, car keys in hand. "I'll start loading the truck. Holler if you need me."

She nodded, watching him disappear down the hall, the weight of the day pressing heavier on her chest.

Before she could gather her thoughts, a soft knock sounded at the door.

When she opened it, she found them—Capri, Charlie Grace, and Lila—standing on the porch, bundled against the morning chill, coffee cups in hand.

"Figured we wouldn't let you get away without one last ambush," Capri said, grinning.

Reva laughed, ushering them inside. "You didn't have to come this early."

Charlie Grace shrugged, her eyes suspiciously bright. "Yeah, we did."

They wandered through the half-empty living room, pausing at boxes ready for the movers marked *Kitchen*, *Books*, *Lucan's Room*.

"Feels weird seeing nearly everything packed up," Lila said softly, trailing her fingers along the mantel where framed photos once stood.

Reva swallowed hard, the ache in her throat sharpening. "Yeah. Feels weird to me, too."

Capri set down her coffee and crossed the room in three strides. She held out a brown paper bag, crumpled and lopsided.

"Found something at the store," she said, a little sheepish. "Figured you might need it."

Reva opened the bag and laughed—a bright red Thunder Mountain baseball cap stared up at her, embroidered with the words *Mountain Tops Forever*.

"You're impossible," Reva said, laughing through the tears she couldn't blink away.

"Don't forget us," Capri said, her voice low.

"Never," Reva promised.

They moved outside to the front yard, where the truck was already half-loaded. Boxes lined the truck bed, the essentials packed carefully among duffels and toys.

Lucan followed them out and sat cross-legged on the driveway, flipping through a picture book. Sweet boy. One of her reasons for going. Her reason for staying brave.

Reva leaned against the tailgate, arms crossed, breathing in the cool mountain air one last time.

Charlie Grace pulled a simple white envelope from her tote bag, her fingers fidgeting with the edge.

"I know I already gave you the photo album with all our photos, including the one of us as kids Lucan brought to the picnic," she said, blushing a little. "But...I couldn't resist giving you one more thing."

Curious, Reva slid her finger under the flap and pulled out a slightly worn photograph. It was their high school graduation picture—Reva, Capri, Charlie Grace, and Lila all grinning under a bright Wyoming sky, their caps crooked, their arms tangled around each other like they never intended to let go.

For a moment, Reva couldn't speak. She ran her thumb lightly over the faded image, the weight of the years pressing soft and sweet against her chest—the memory of them getting ready for the graduation ceremony forming, causing her throat to squeeze even more with emotion.

Charlie Grace smiled. "Just in case you ever forget where you belong."

Reva blinked hard and tucked the photo carefully back into the envelope. "Not a chance."

They laughed, and for a heartbeat, it felt like everything was normal again.

Lila stepped forward next, her hands twisting nervously.

"I have something too," she said, pressing a tiny box into Reva's palm.

Inside was a delicate gold pendant—four hearts intertwined, gleaming in the morning light.

"The four of us remain," Lila said, voice trembling. "No matter where life takes us. Forever friends."

Reva closed her fingers around the necklace, holding it to her chest. Words failed her. Only the fierce thump of love remained.

"I don't deserve y'all," she whispered.

"That's where you're wrong," Capri said, fiercely. "We're the fortunate ones. And you deserve everything good."

They stood there, four women bound not by blood, but by choice, by years of laughter and tears, by fights and forgiveness and showing up—always showing up.

The time to leave crept closer.

Reva helped Kellen secure the final boxes they were taking in their vehicle—those items too precious to risk losing in the transport. Capri fastened the bungee cords. Charlie Grace snapped a few last photos—Lucan clambering into the backseat, Kellen adjusting the rearview mirror.

When there was nothing left to load, no more errands to distract her, Reva turned back to them.

This was it.

Capri stepped forward first, yanking Reva into a hug so fierce it nearly knocked the wind out of her.

"You better call when you get there," Capri muttered into her shoulder. "I don't care if it's two a.m."

"I will," Reva promised.

Charlie Grace hugged her next, lingering for a long moment. "You taught me how to stand on my own two feet when it mattered most," she whispered. "Now it's our turn to stand steady for you."

And finally Lila, who simply pressed her face against Reva's shoulder and cried.

"I'm so proud of you," she whispered. "So proud."

Reva kissed the top of her head, holding her tight. "I'm proud of all of us."

They pulled apart reluctantly, blinking fast against the tears that threatened to unravel everything.

Capri sniffed and jabbed a finger toward the road. "You'd better get moving before I tackle you back into the house."

Reva laughed, climbing into the front passenger's seat.

At the last minute, Charlie Grace pulled something from

her pocket—a simple white envelope. She handed it to Reva through the window. "Open this when you get to Georgia and get settled."

Reva tucked it carefully into her jacket pocket. "What is it?"

Charlie Grace grinned. "Emergency plan." She paused. "Don't ask details. Just open it later." She leaned and brushed Reva's cheek with a kiss, then stepped back.

Lucan waved wildly from the back. "Bye, Aunt Capri! Bye, Aunt Charlie! Bye, Aunt Lila!"

The three women waved back, shouting goodbyes, promises, and I-love-yous.

Kellen nodded his goodbye and started the engine. The truck rumbled to life, a sound so final it made Reva's chest ache.

She gripped her purse, hesitating.

One last look.

Through the windshield, she saw them standing in the driveway—Capri with her fists on her hips, Charlie Grace dabbing her eyes, Lila blowing kisses.

These women were indeed forever friends.

As the truck rolled forward, Charlie Grace suddenly darted into the yard and grabbed a handful of wildflowers. She flung them into the air, petals spinning like confetti against the rising sun.

Capri and Lila joined in, plucking handfuls and tossing them high, laughing and crying and waving wildly.

Petals rained down around them, bright against the gray gravel drive, a living memory Reva would carry forever.

Tears blurred her vision as she rolled down the window and waved back, heart thudding with the weight of love and loss and gratitude so big it filled every corner of her soul.

The house shrank in the rearview mirror, and before long, the town slipped into the folds of the mountains.

But Reva knew, deep and certain, that she wasn't leaving anything behind.

The best parts of Thunder Mountain—the laughter, the loyalty, the fierce, stubborn love—were stitched into her now, woven through every beat of her heart.

Wherever life took her next, she would never be alone.

Where roots run deep, the heart finds its way home.

Always.

29

Three months later

The porch lights flanking the entrance cast a warm amber glow over the front steps of Sunnyside Acres. Reva rocked slowly in a weathered chair, a glass of sweet tea sweating in her hand, the wooden floorboards creaking beneath her boots.

Out on the wide lawn, Lucan darted barefoot after fireflies, his laughter floating up into the thick Georgia twilight. Beyond the old pecan grove, the trees stretched toward the darkening horizon, their leaves whispering secrets in the soft night breeze, timeless and sure.

Home.

It still felt new on her tongue, like a word she was learning how to say.

But every day it settled a little deeper into her bones.

Grand Memaw's house had always been beautiful, its charm never fading with the years. Once quiet and heavy with memory, it now brimmed with new life. Kellen had spent weekends refreshing the front steps, while Reva had brightened the shutters herself, laughing when Lucan flung blue paint across both of them. Together, they were filling Sunnyside Acres with energy and joy, one small project at a time.

And along the way, her heart was filling up, too.

Her phone buzzed on the side table beside her. Reva smiled, already knowing who it would be.

Charlie Grace: *"Don't forget — Friends Are Forever Night begins in five minutes!"*

Reva chuckled, setting down her glass and reaching for the tablet Kellen had rigged up for video calls.

Every Saturday night since she'd left, the four of them had gathered on a video call, no matter what chaos life threw their way. Kids, husbands, ranch emergencies—it didn't matter. They showed up.

That was the promise.

And they were keeping it.

The screen flickered, and suddenly Capri's face filled the frame, wearing a baseball cap and grinning wide.

"Hey, city slicker," Capri teased. "You growin' pecans yet, or just drinking all the sweet tea in Georgia?"

"Both," Reva laughed, angling the camera toward the orchard. "These trees are older than Thunder Mountain itself."

Charlie Grace popped onto the screen next, fiddling with her camera angle, a dog barking in the background.

"Guess what?" she said breathlessly. "One of my photographs made it into the Jackson Hole exhibit! First place."

Cheers erupted from everyone. Reva clapped, beaming with pride. "Well deserved, friend," she said. "Told you the world needed your eyes."

Charlie Grace flushed pink. "Couldn't have done it without all of your encouragement."

Then Lila joined, balancing a cup of tea and waving with her free hand.

"Camille's internship just got extended," she said, settling into her chair. "She's doing great. And Whit and I...we're thinking about adding another exam room to the clinic. Business is booming."

More cheers, more laughter.

For an hour, they caught up on everything and nothing—the latest town gossip, Lila's stubborn new goat who ate through her daisy patch, Capri's new idea to start "Sunset Tours" on the river. The upcoming election for mayor. A lopsided election given there was only one candidate—Jake Carrington.

"My husband can rebuild anything," Capri noted. "Even Thunder Mountain after the loss of Reva."

At some point, Charlie Grace leaned closer to her screen and said, mock-stern, "And don't you dare think we've forgotten your birthday next month. Gifts incoming."

Reva laughed. "You girls don't need to—"

"Stop," Charlie Grace said, pointing a finger. "It's happening. Deal with it."

Reva raised both hands in surrender. "All right, all right."

Their laughter filled the night air, as rich and vibrant as if they were sitting right beside her.

When they finally said good night—after promising, yet again, to text first thing tomorrow—Reva sat back in the rocker, the house quiet except for the creak of wood and the far-off chirp of crickets.

The stars blinked awake overhead, dusting the velvet sky with light.

Reva tucked the tablet back onto the side table and picked up the envelope Charlie Grace had made her promise not to open until she was fully settled. She ran her thumb over the soft paper before sliding her finger under the flap.

Inside was a single sheet, handwritten in Charlie Grace's looping script.

. . .

Emergency Reunion Protocol
1. If missing friends becomes unbearable, text "*Code Red.*"
2. Immediate response required: video call, meme exchange, or flights booked.
3. No apologies allowed for crying.
4. Laughter is mandatory.
5. Wherever we are—wherever you are—friends are forever.

Tears pricked her eyes, blurring the neat lines of ink.

Reva folded the paper carefully and slipped it into the pocket of her jacket—the same worn one she'd chosen to wear at the town's goodbye party. Somehow, the fabric still smelled faintly of smoke and wildflowers.

She stood, stepping off the porch into the cool night.

The stars above Georgia looked different than the stars above Thunder Mountain. But they were still stars. Still part of the same great sky.

And she was still Reva Nygard—still stitched to her people by bonds too strong for distance to sever.

She had roots here now, sinking into the rich Georgia soil, twining alongside those old pecan trees.

But her heart? A big piece of her heart remained in the Teton Mountains.

In the distance, Lucan whooped as he caught another firefly, his joy echoing across the fields.

Kellen called from the other end of the porch, holding out a hand. "Come inside, honey."

Reva smiled and turned back toward the house—her house, her new life—her heart so full it was a wonder it didn't lift her straight off the ground.

As she crossed the porch threshold, she paused and looked back at the night sky one last time.

And in a voice soft and sure, she whispered the words that had carried her this far—and would carry her for many years to come.

Charlie Grace, Lila, Capri.

They truly were friends forever.

AUTHOR'S NOTE

Hello, Readers!

A heartfelt thank you for reading the Teton Mountain Series. These books celebrate the invaluable role of friendships. I am thankful to have girlfriends I've known since high school. These women bless me beyond what I can describe.

The spark for these stories was my own experiences of profound friendship, a theme I've always wanted to explore in my writing.

A trip to Yellowstone National Park and the Teton Mountain National Park in Wyoming inspired the setting. For any of you who have followed me, you know I thrill to take my readers to places I love to vacation. In these books, you'll be whisked away to the majestic Teton Mountains, you'll dine in the trendy restaurants in Jackson Hole, and see bears and moose in secluded pinewood forests. You'll experience herds of buffalo roaming the meadows of Hayden Valley and hike the backcountry trails around crystal blue lakes lined with pastel-colored lupine blooms. The town of Thunder Mountain is a fictionalized community based upon DuBois, Wyoming—a charming western town with wooden boardwalks and quaint buildings lining its Main Street. I took a little liberty as an author and relocated it to where Moran is now on the map.

Mostly, I created four women friends who have become so very dear to me as I've placed them on the pages of these books—Charlie Grace, Reva, Lila and Capri.

I hope you enjoy the time spent with us!

Kellie Coates Gilbert

ABOUT THE AUTHOR

USA Today Bestselling Author Kellie Coates Gilbert has won readers' hearts with her heartwarming and highly emotional stories about women and the relationships that define their lives. As a former legal investigator, Kellie brings a unique blend of insight and authenticity to her stories, ensuring that readers are hooked from the very first page.

In addition to garnering hundreds of five-star reviews, Kellie has been described by RT Book Reviews as a "deft, crisp storyteller." Her books were featured as Barnes & Noble Top Shelf Picks and earned a coveted place on Library Journal's Best Book List.

Born and raised amidst the breathtaking beauty of Sun Valley, Idaho, Kellie draws inspiration from the vibrant landscapes of her youth, infusing her stories with a vivid sense of place. Kellie now lives with her husband of over thirty-five years in Dallas, where she spends most days by her pool drinking sweet tea and writing the stories of her heart.

Learn more about Kellie and her books at www.kelliecoatesgilbert.com

Enjoy special discounts by buying direct from Kellie at www.kelliecoatesgilbertbooks.com

ALSO BY KELLIE COATES GILBERT

Dear Readers,

Thank you for reading this story. If you'd like to read more of my books, please check out these series. To purchase at special discounts: www.kelliecoatesgilbertbooks.com

TETON MOUNTAIN SERIES

Where We Belong – Book 1

Echoes of the Heart – Book 2

Holding the Dream – Book 3

As the Sun Rises – Book 4

Losing the Moon – Book 5

Friends are Forever – Book 6

A Teton Mountain Christmas – Book 7

MAUI ISLAND SERIES

Under the Maui Sky – Book 1

Silver Island Moon – Book 2

Tides of Paradise – Book 3

The Last Aloha – Book 4

Ohana Sunrise – Book 5

Sweet Plumeria Dawn – Book 6

Songs of the Rainbow – Book 7

Hibiscus Christmas – Book 8

PACIFIC BAY SERIES

Chances Are – Book 1

Remember Us – Book 2

Chasing Wind – Book 3

Between Rains – Book 4

SUN VALLEY SERIES

Sisters – Book 1

Heartbeats – Book 2

Changes – Book 3

Promises – Book 4

TEXAS GOLD COLLECTION

A Woman of Fortune – Book 1

Where Rivers Part – Book 2

A Reason to Stay – Book 3

What Matters Most – Book 4

STAND ALONE NOVELS:

Mother of Pearl

AVAILABLE AT ALL MAJOR RETAILERS

FOR EXCLUSIVE DISCOUNTS:

www.kelliecoatesgilbertbooks.com

SNEEK PEEK - SISTERS (SUN VALLEY SERIES BOOK 1)

Chapter 1

Karyn Macadam slowed her car as the sign to the Hemingway Memorial came into view. She turned off Sun Valley Road into the parking area, not bothering to signal. There was no need, not at this early hour.

Cutting the engine, she sat quietly for a few moments, the radio blaring in the background.

And we expect another warm summer day here in the Wood River Valley as residents in this popular resort area prepare to commemorate one of its own, nearly a year and a half after the tragic accident that took the life of—

Karyn shut off the radio, her heart thudding painfully.

Squeezing the steering wheel, she refused to look at the seat next to her—at the small wooden box intricately carved with falling snowflakes over a set of crossed skis.

Deep breath in. Deep breath out.

Five more minutes she sat there, putting off what was ahead.

Finally, she scooped the box into her hands and climbed out of the car.

She'd made a promise. One she fully intended to keep, even if she'd made it a bit tongue-in-cheek at the time.

Gravel crunched beneath her feet as she traversed the walkway toward the memorial. Even in the faint morning light she could make out wild poppies and blue flax, delicate against the pungent skunk cabbage jutting from the pebbled ground lining the trail.

The sound of water bubbling across a rocky streambed pulled her toward the monument nested against a stand of aspen trees, their tiny dollar-shaped leaves barely moving in the still air.

It was understandable why the famous novelist had loved Idaho, why he'd spent his last days living here. Ernest Hemingway was only one of many celebrities who had traded big city tangled traffic for cool mountain mornings and alpine vistas and made Sun Valley their residence.

Olympic hopeful Dean Macadam was another.

Karyn stood at the water's edge and looked past the pile of flat stones with its stately column rising from the middle, beyond the trees to the golf course in the distance. A deer standing in the middle of one of the greens lifted its head and stared back at her in mutual regard.

A voice in her head rang out as clear as if Dean were standing next to her.

"What is your fascination with Hemingway anyway?"

She closed her eyes, remembered gazing up from the pages of *For Whom the Bell Tolls*. "Are you crazy? He was only the best American novelist of all time," she'd so flippantly reminded her husband.

Dean playfully tugged at the sheet tucked around her bare waist. "Is that so?"

She quickly snatched the covering from his hands and

secured it more tightly. "Yes, that's so. In fact, Ernest Hemingway is known for his mastery of theme and imagery. Take this story for example." She held up the heavy volume borrowed from her dad, its cover worn from repeated readings. "The entire narrative is punctuated with a preoccupation with death and dying, which is so poignant given his eventual suicide."

Dean ran broad fingers through his sleep-tousled hair. "Yeah, you see—that's what I don't get. Why is so many people's imagination captured with a guy who spent an inordinate amount of time writing about life instead of living it? I mean, in my view, that's likely what led to him offing himself in the end."

She raised her gaze in horror and slammed the book against her new husband's chest. "Don't say that."

He laughed. "Okay, okay—look, I get it. Ernest Hemingway is your book boyfriend. I'm not jealous. Really I'm not." His eyes nearly sparkled when he'd said that. "Tell you what. When I die, you just take my ashes and toss them in that little creek that runs in front of his memorial. That way, when I'm gone, you can visit both of us at the same time."

Before she could protest the macabre suggestion, he pulled the novel from her and tossed it to the floor, while at the same time lifting the sheet with his other hand.

She'd giggled as he buried his head against her skin. "Promise me. Even if my mother protests and wants otherwise," he said, in a muffled voice. "Now. Promise. Or, I'll—" His fingers dug into her sides and he tickled, sending her entire torso into a fit of squirming. "Promise," he repeated.

"I promise. I promise," she shouted, laughing uncontrollably.

He immediately stopped tickling. "Okay, that's better." Her new husband looked at her then, his eyes boring into her soul. "And promise you'll always remember I love you."

The sound of his voice still seemed so real, even after all

these months. She sunk to the curved stone bench. Tears collected in her eyes and spilled over, making their way down her cheeks. She fingered the familiar lid on the box.

I'm sorry, Dean. I can't do it.

No matter that she'd gotten out of her bed while it was still dark outside with the best intentions. She still wasn't ready to let him go.

Not now—and maybe never.

***

Grayson Chandler wrangled his way past a bunch of willow branches, taking care not to break his fly rod, then headed south crossing into a clearing.

That's when he saw her.

Early thirties. Coffee-colored long hair. Sitting quietly on the stone bench at the Hemingway Memorial.

Not really understanding why, he quieted his steps as he approached.

She held something in her hands, a little box. Her head was tucked. Was she—?

Holding his breath, he moved closer.

Yes, she was crying.

He crouched behind a clump of thick brush and watched, knowing he was encroaching, but unable to help himself.

She was a pretty gal. Frankly, she reminded him a whole lot of that royal lady in England. What was her name? Not Princess Diana, but her son's wife.

Unable to remember, he shook his head. Didn't matter.

What mattered was that she was openly weeping now.

He wavered. Should he step forward? Offer her assistance? He shook his head. Naw—probably not. It wasn't like he carried a handkerchief in his pocket like his dad used to. Likely she just needed some time to get whatever was bothering her out of her system. Women were like that.

Still, he couldn't help but think whatever she was spilling

about was not the least bit inconsequential. Clearly, she was torn up.

Ignoring the reprimanding voice inside that warned him he was being voyeuristic, he rested his fly pole on the ground and continued to watch.

Even crying, she was beautiful, what with her thick lashes sweeping across ivory cheeks that looked as soft as a rose petal. He knotted his hand and pressed it against his lips, imagining brushing his thumb across her skin.

He hadn't thought about a woman in that way for a really long time. Not since—well, since Robin. A subject he didn't care to think about.

The woman on the bench wiped her face with the back of her hand and looked up toward the sky. A few seconds later, she fingered the top of the little wooden box in her lap, chewing at her lip.

Finally, she stood and gazed into the trees, tears still rimming her lashes.

He battled a surge of protectiveness, yet remained still. Under different circumstances he might take a chance, go introduce himself. But he knew better this time.

She turned and saw him. Frowning, she pulled the little box close to her chest.

Face flushed, he reached for his pole and stood. "Hey, I'm sorry. I didn't mean to—what I meant is, I just didn't want to interrupt—" He shook his head. "Look, I'm sorry."

Judging from the way she fidgeted, she too was embarrassed. She tucked a strand of hair behind her ear. "I—I thought I was alone."

"I wasn't really watching. I was doing a little fly fishing." He pointed back at the creek. "I saw you and—"

She rubbed at the place between her eyebrows, then dropped her hand. "Look, I really need to go." She turned and starting walking toward the parking lot.

He wanted to say something more, maybe get her name, but thought better of it.

Upon reaching her car, she glanced back.

In an awkward attempt to apologize again for his intrusion on her private moments, he nodded and gave her a faint smile.

Inside, he wanted to kick himself.

Want to read more? Visit my website where you'll find links to all retailers and format options.

www.kelliecoatesgilbert.com

SNEEK PEAK - UNDER THE MAUI SKY (MAUI ISLAND SERIES BOOK 1)

Chapter 1

Ava Briscoe took a deep breath and leaned into the bamboo-framed mirror above the sink. "Goodness," she thought. "This dress and pearls make me look so...tired." Normally, she wore comfortable, loose-fitted garments, happy and bright-colored. Her half of the closet was filled with tropical prints, linen trousers she loved to roll at the ankle, and flip-flops. Over twenty pairs were lined up on the floor, yet she often slipped into the same favorite pair—soft-sole black Reefs.

She pulled the tube of lipstick to her mouth, then leaned a little closer. As Ava drew the color over her lips, she couldn't help but notice the dark circles under her eyes. No amount of that miracle product she'd ordered online had erased the telltale signs that she hadn't slept in days.

"Mom?" Christel peeked her head through the bathroom door. "I think it's about time."

Ava smiled weakly back at her oldest daughter and pushed the lid back on her lipstick tube. "Okay."

"You alright, Mom?"

Ava forced a brightness in her voice. "Sure, honey. No need to worry." She moved to join her daughter at the door, smoothed her dress. "I just want to see your dad a minute first."

Christel slowly nodded. "Yeah, okay. Sure. Want me to go with—"

"No," Ava quickly assured her. "I'll join you in a minute."

Christel nodded a second time. "Okay. I love you, Mom."

"I love you, too, baby." Ava turned and took one final glance in the mirror and pressed a stray curl back in place before heading out the door.

Only a few people lingered in the church foyer as she walked across the tiled floor past the open double doors leading outside to the gardens. A slight breeze carried the scent of plumeria and white ginger and blew that stray curl out of place again. Ava gave up and tucked the rogue piece of hair behind her ear for good measure.

Wailea Seaside Chapel was located on Molokini Bluff, with breathtaking ocean views and luxurious grounds. The chapel was like something out of a fairy tale and featured soaring rafters, hand-carved wooden pews, and stained-glass windows. She and Lincoln had been married here, as had her younger daughter, Katie.

A ukulele played from inside the chapel where the others were gathered. She couldn't help herself. The corners of her lips turned up slightly as she recognized her favorite song—"Somewhere Over the Rainbow". The version by Israel Kamakawiwo'ole, or Iz, as people on the island called him.

Her hand reached for the knob on the closed door to the right of the potted Bromeliad plant. She pushed the door ajar slightly, listened to make sure only her husband was in the room. Detecting no one, she entered.

"Lincoln, can you hear that? They're playing our song," she said as she neared her husband. She reached and straightened his tie, then pulled the lapels of that awful suit into alignment. "Remember? That was the song that was playing that first night at the Grand Wailea."

Ava had been less than twenty years old when she'd met Lincoln Briscoe at her best friend's wedding. She was the maid of honor. Lincoln, the best man.

From the moment she laid eyes on him, her focus was scattered, so filled with nervous anticipation, even giddy. When they were seated next to each other at the luau reception, she couldn't even hold a conversation. Her thoughts danced in infinite directions as they lifted glasses in a toast to their friends, the newly married couple. As their glass clinked, she could picture the scene already—the two of them holding hands on their first date. He would take her for a long, bare-footed walk on Mokapu Beach and watch the sunset behind craggy black rocks and towering palms.

Amazing thing? It had been just like that.

Of course, years of marriage had rubbed the shine off a bit. Raising four children and running a pineapple plantation could do that to a couple. Even so, their marriage had remained solid, reliable. They loved each other. For that, she was grateful.

"Well, honey. I guess it's time." An uninvited tear rolled down Ava's cheek. Fighting to breathe, she leaned and kissed her husband's forehead.

For the last time.

"Thank you, Lincoln," she whispered close to his ear. "You made me very happy. I—Well, I loved you more than I can say." She choked back a sob and straightened. Now was not the time. There would be months, even years, ahead to miss this man— the man she'd shared her life with.

Lincoln was gone. She wasn't sure how she was going to go on without him.

She swept her hand across his chest, gave a final pat.

It was then she noticed a tiny corner from a piece of paper

peeking out from the pocket of Lincoln's jacket. Ava scowled with curiosity and tugged the note free, opened it. Scrawled across the paper were the words *Ua ola loko i ke aloha.*

She scowled.

Who in the world had placed the note in her husband's pocket? One of the children, perhaps? And what did the words mean?

After living on Maui for as long as she had, Ava had assimilated into Hawaiian culture to some extent, yet her vocabulary still remained somewhat limited.

"Ava. Sweet *hoaloha*. Are you ready?"

She turned to see her closest friend peeking her head inside the door, her face filled with sympathy. "It's time," her friend said gently.

Ava mustered a weak nod. "Yes, Alani. I'm ready." Ava lifted her chin, bit at her trembling lip. Somehow the words didn't make their way to her heart. She was anything but ready.

She tucked the note inside her bag. With one final look back over her shoulder, she followed her friend out the door.

Want to read more? Visit my website where you'll find links to all retailers and format options.

www.kelliecoatesgilbert.com

Made in the USA
Monee, IL
03 August 2025